DISCAR
URBANA I
S0-CFF-530

Wife

Extraordinaire

The Urbana Free Library

To renew: call 217-367-4057
or go to "*urbanafreelibrary.org*"
and select "Renew/Request Items"

DISCARDED BY THE
OZEANA FREE LIBRARY

Also by Kiki Swinson

Playing Dirty
Notorious
Wifey
I'm Still Wifey
Life After Wifey
Still Wifey Material
A Sticky Situation
The Candy Shop
Wife Extraordinaire
Wife Extraordinaire Returns

Anthologies
Sleeping with the Enemy (with Wahida Clark)
Heist (with De'nesha Diamond)
Lifestyles of the Rich and Shameless (with Noire)
A Gangster and a Gentleman (with De'nesha Diamond)
Most Wanted (with Nikki Turner)
Still Candy Shopping (with Amaleka McCall)
Fistful of Benjamins (with De'nesha Diamond)

Published by Kensington Publishing Corp.

Wife
Extraordinaire

Kiki
Swinson

Kensington Publishing Corp.
http://www.kensingtonbooks.com

DAFINA BOOKS are published by

Kensington Publishing Corp.
119 West 40th Street
New York, NY 10018

Copyright © 2014 by Kiki Swinson

All rights reserved. No part of this book may be reproduced in any form or by any means without the prior written consent of the Publisher, excepting brief quotes used in reviews.

If you purchased this book without a cover, you should be aware that this book is stolen property. It was reported as "unsold and destroyed" to the Publisher and neither the Author nor the Publisher has received any payment for this "stripped book."

All Kensington Titles, Imprints, and Distributed Lines are available at special quantity discounts for bulk purchases for sales promotions, premiums, fund-raising, and educational or institutional use. Special book excerpts or customized printings can also be created to fit specific needs. For details, write or phone the office of the Kensington special sales manager: Kensington Publishing Corp., 119 West 40th Street, New York, NY 10018, attn: Special Sales Department, Phone: 1-800-221-2647.

Dafina and the Dafina logo Reg. U.S. Pat. & TM Off.

ISBN-13: 978-0-7582-9379-4
ISBN-10: 0-7582-9379-8
First Dafina Mass Market Edition: June 2014

10 9 8 7 6 5 4 3 2 1

Printed in the United States of America

Wife
Extraordinaire

1

Trice

I was a nervous wreck about the arrangement my husband, Troy, made with his homeboy, Leon Bunch, when he agreed to swap me for his wife and be filmed for a reality TV show. I would soon learn to take the bitter with the sweet. I mean, it wasn't like it was the end of the world. The terms were simple. I was only going to swap lives with Leon's wife for a period of seven days for a show called *Trading Wives*, which was similar to the reality shows *Wife Swap* and *Trading Spouses*, which were already hit shows playing on television. The only difference with what we were doing versus the other two shows was that we wouldn't have a camera crew following us around. The show's executives had the production crew install cameras throughout our houses several days ago so that all the footage they needed would be recorded with those cameras.

It wouldn't be long before all of our dirty laundry would be aired out on television at a much later date.

To compensate us for selling our souls, they would pay both couples ten thousand dollars each at the end of the seventh day. Getting paid ten grand was music to our ears. I couldn't speak for the other couple, but I knew Troy and I had a few bills we needed to take care of. Besides that, Troy was the only breadwinner in our house, and I knew that extra money would take some strain off him.

Troy was my rock. So much so, I'd do anything for him. And if it meant that I had to live in someone else's house, then I was there. While I was there, I vowed that I'd concentrate on the big payday, so I should be all right in the end.

Troy warned his friend Leon that I was accustomed to a certain kind of living. I was a little brat. But all I knew about Leon was that he was a mechanic in the service department at a Nissan dealership in Chesapeake, while his wife, Charlene, was a stay-at-home mom with their five-year-old son. My life was somewhat similar to Charlene's life. She and I both were stay-at-home wives. The only difference with our employment status was that I volunteered my services to a nonprofit organization twice a week and Charlene was a reformed stripper who retired and now she sat around at home and waited on handouts from her husband, Leon.

Troy and I had a nice three-bedroom home in the Pine Crest neighborhood of Virginia Beach, while Leon and Charlene's town house sat in the Norview area of Norfolk. When people thought about the Norview area of Norfolk, they thought of the ghetto, the hood. So I knew I was going to spend a lot of my time inside the house.

"Trice, do you have all your things packed?" Troy asked me.

I had just zipped up the last compartment of my luggage when Troy appeared before me. I stood by the bed and looked directly at him. "Yeah, I think so," I finally said after I looked at him from head to toe.

I had to admit that my husband was one handsome guy. He was five eleven, with a nice build and light skin complexion. He was definitely a pretty boy. I sure loved my man. He sort of reminded me of the actor Michael Ealy who played Chris Brown's older brother in the movie *Takers,* opposite of rapper T.I. and Idris Elba. We'd been together for more than seven years, so we were thick as thieves, which was why I went along with this whole setup. In my own twisted mind, I felt like this would be a good experience and I could probably take something from it. So after I assured Troy that all my things were packed, he helped me carry everything to his truck.

"Are you nervous?" he asked me after he placed my luggage inside the truck.

"Not really. But I do feel a little weird staying at your homeboy's house," I replied, and then I sat down in the passenger seat and closed the door behind myself.

Troy climbed into the driver's seat and closed his door. "Leon ain't just my homeboy—he's like a brother to me. Trust me, he's going to make sure you're all right."

Troy turned on the ignition, put his black F-150 into drive, and then sped off. As he drove away from our house, I took one last look at it because I knew it would be seven days before I saw it again.

The ride to Norfolk didn't take long at all. Troy and I talked about the dos and don'ts the entire drive. And before I got out of the truck, I laid down a few rules myself. Just like the TV show, I instructed him to make her sleep in the guest room. I also instructed him to make sure she walked around in presentable attire. And before he went to bed at night, he needed to call me. He promised me that he would take care of everything and that I had absolutely nothing to worry about.

"We're here," he pointed out as soon as we

pulled up in front of a tan, vinyl-sided duplex on Chesapeake Boulevard.

I looked at the building and then I looked back at my husband. "I sure hope the inside is much cleaner than the outside."

Troy cracked a smile. "They keep a decent, clean house, so you'll be fine."

I gave him a nonchalant expression. "Yeah, they better," I commented, and then I leaned forward to kiss him on the lips.

After our lips parted, I turned back around to open the passenger door. Before I could make my exit, I noticed a video-vixen-looking chick walking in our direction. I figured it had to be Leon's wife, Charlene. "Is that your friend's wife?" I asked Troy.

"Yeah, that's her," he replied after he looked past me.

I took a good look at Charlene as she walked toward Troy and me. I had to admit, she was an attractive woman. She looked to be a size twelve, which was one size bigger than I was, but she was shapely. Her hair was short, but it was cut nicely into a Chinese bob. I could instantly tell that her hair was a weave because it was too shiny and straight to be her own. Black people don't have that texture of hair. The Korean who sold her that hair played her like a fiddle. Charlene was too dark for it and they knew it.

I had the perfect light skin complexion. Not to mention I had beautiful hazel-colored eyes. So if she and I stood side by side, all eyes would be on me. She had absolutely nothing on me and I'm convinced that my husband would see that too. If anything, she needed to be worried about her husband trying to mess around with me. I was a force to be reckoned with, so she'd better be careful.

She walked up to the truck showing all her damn teeth. "How y'all doing?" she asked. I didn't say a word, but I smiled. Troy returned the greeting and then he introduced us. She extended her right hand and I shook it.

Her husband, Leon, came behind her. I looked over her shoulder to get a good look at him. He wasn't my type in the least bit, so Troy had absolutely nothing to worry about. However, Leon did seem really cool. He smiled from ear to ear when he saw Troy. "What's good, nigga?"

Troy reached over me to shake Leon's hands. After they shook, I eased out of the truck so Charlene could put her things in the backseat.

"You ladies ready to see that the grass ain't greener on the other side?" Leon spoke up.

"I never said it was!" Charlene answered first.

"Well, I'm just going along for the ride. Who knows, I might just learn something from it," I replied.

Leon took my two pieces of luggage from my hands. I expressed my gratitude while Troy watched Charlene shove her bags into the backseat. I looked at him and shook my head. He sure knew how to be lazy.

"You better take care of my wife!" Troy told Leon.

"Oh, she's in good hands. So, you better do the same thing," Leon replied.

Troy gave Leon a smirk. "Oh, don't worry. When this is all over, she's going to come back home and tell you about all the shit I schooled her on."

Leon threw his hands up. "Yeah, whatever, nigga! We shall see," he commented, and he and I watched as Troy pulled off in his black Ford F-150.

After Troy disappeared, Leon turned to me and asked, "Are you ready?"

I smiled at him and said, "I guess I am."

Once we were inside his duplex, I immediately noticed a strong smell of bleach and ammonia. He walked ahead of me. We made our way down a short hallway that led to the kitchen and an open family room with a fifty-two-inch flat-screen TV. After I entered the den area, I took a seat on the sofa and laid my things down on the floor next to me. I glanced around the room. Every picture they had nailed on the wall looked very cheap. The furniture I was sitting on was in even more bad taste. *Swap meet* was written on every piece of décor they had in this house.

"Where is your son?" I wondered aloud. I didn't want to make it obvious about how badly their house was decorated, so I tried to start up a general conversation.

"My wife's parents just picked him up last night so he could spend the summer with them in Florida."

"Wow! Florida sounds nice. I know he's gonna have fun while he's there."

Leon closed the mini-blinds on the front windows in the den area. After he finished, he looked at me and asked, "Are you ready for me to show you where you'll be sleeping?"

"Sure. Why not?" I said, and stood to my feet.

He grabbed my bags from the floor and led the way. I followed him up a flight of stairs to the second floor. He stopped at the first room on the left. Before we entered, he looked back and informed me that we were about to enter his son's bedroom.

This is where I'll be sleeping? "Oh, okay. That's fine," I assured him, even though I didn't have a good feeling about the way he was going about this.

Leon smiled and pushed the door open. I walked into the bedroom behind him. I immediately surveyed my surroundings and noticed how decorative this little boy's room was. The theme of the bedroom was World Wrestling Champions. He had professional wrestling figures on his dresser with matching curtains, comforters, sheets, pillowcases, and a throw rug. It was really cute, so it made me smile.

Leon set my bags on top of his son's bed. "If you need anything, make sure you let me know."

I assured him I would. And when he left the bedroom, he closed the door behind him.

I took a seat on the twin-size bed and reflected on my decision to go along with this plan of theirs. I also wondered what my husband was doing and if he'd gotten home yet. My mind would not allow me to play the guessing game, so I grabbed my cell phone from my purse and dialed his number. He answered my call on the second ring. The music coming from the speakers of his truck was extremely loud, so I found myself yelling through the receiver.

"Why do you have the music playing so loud?" I screamed.

" 'Cause my song is on," he screamed back. "Baby, you know I like this new joint by Jay-Z."

I sighed. "You know I'm beginning to miss you already."

"Damn, Trice, we've only been apart for ten minutes."

"I know, but the thought of us being away from each other for one whole week got me a little sad."

"Come on now, you a big girl. Everything is going to be all right. I mean, it ain't like we won't be able to speak to one another. So just call me every time you get lonely."

I sucked my teeth and sighed once more. "It's not the same, though."

"I know. But seven days isn't long, so as soon as you blink your eyes, those days are gonna fly right by."

"Easy for you to say."

"Come on, Trice, you a soldier. And besides, look at this vacation away from each other as a ten-thousand-dollar investment. Now, suck it up and call me back before you go to bed. Okay, baby?"

"Yeah. All right," I replied nonchalantly, and then I pressed the END button.

After I hung up, I got myself together and headed back downstairs. Leon was in the den area, watching the news on the TV when I walked in. He was not just watching the news, he was engrossed in it. I had the chance to look at him from another angle. He wasn't as handsome as Troy, but he had unique features. He was dark skinned with dark brown eyes. His hair was locked with shoulder-length dreads, which was unattractive to me. Long hair on men was not my cup of tea. But for some reason, it looked okay on him. It had to be because he had naturally curly hair at the root. His choice in attire was cool. I honestly liked how he coordinated his yellow Lacoste polo shirt with his acid-washed True Religion jeans. Troy told me he was a mechanic, but from the looks of his hands, it seemed impossible because this guy's hands were well manicured.

"Hungry?" he asked me.

"Not really," I replied, and then I took a seat down on the sofa next to him.

Leon rubbed his stomach in a circular motion and said, "Well, I am. So I'm gonna order me a pizza with some hot wings."

Before I could utter a word, he stood up and grabbed his iPhone from the end table next to the lamp. I took it that he had Papa John's Pizza on speed dial because he only pressed one button from the touch pad of his phone and then I heard it ring. After he placed his order, he hung up and walked out of the room.

"Want something to drink?" he yelled.

"No. I'm fine."

"You sure? Because I got juice, bottled water, and cold beer."

"Yes, I'm sure," I assured him.

Ten seconds later, he reappeared with a cold and refreshing-looking bottle of Corona in his hand. After he sat back down, he grabbed the remote and surfed through the channels until he came across the sitcom *Two and a Half Men*.

"I love this show. Charlie Sheen and that little boy are funny as hell."

"Yeah, they are," I commented.

We both sat there and watched the show. It quickly became apparent that he was somewhat cool with a sense of humor. So I relaxed a little more and hoped that these days would go by very quickly.

I had never been away from Troy for more than a couple of days. And even then, it was hard. Troy was my protector and more. He made sure I had everything I needed and he never questioned my motives. The secret to our happiness was that we kept it real with one another. Lying to each other wasn't an option. From day one, we vowed that if temptation ever crept in our minds that we'd be honest about it and bring it to the other's attention so we could handle it immediately.

I can't speak on how Leon and Charlene handled their differences, but I will say that after this *Trading Wives* arrangement was over, I'd have the answers.

2

Troy

Trice didn't know it, but it was all my idea to swap Leon's wife for her. Leon owed me from a bet on last week's NBA finals game, so he either had to kick off one grand or relieve me of my wife for seven days. Don't get me wrong, I loved my wife. But Trice could be a difficult woman to live with at times. She nagged me about everything I did. I never did anything right if you asked her. She wanted everything around the house to be perfect. So if I left my clothes on the floor in the bathroom or left my dishes in the kitchen sink overnight, she blew up about it and I would hear about it for at least another twenty-four hours. Not to mention I had to damn near get on my knees to beg her to fuck me. I didn't get my dick sucked at all, so I made it my business not to ask. She had this phobia of putting my meat in her mouth. When I asked her about it, she would never give me an explanation.

Over the past seven years, I could honestly say the first three years were good. But the last four had been a complete nightmare. My marriage was falling apart by the seams, and she refused to acknowledge it. I wasn't happy anymore, which was why I opted for Leon to let his wife stay here. I needed to see if the grass was greener on the other side. Leon's wife didn't know he was about to file for a divorce. He was tired of her more than I was of Trice. So you see, this arrangement would benefit both of us. But I guess we would see in the end.

"You and your wife have a nice home," Charlene expressed after I took her on a tour of the house.

I smiled as I escorted her back into the kitchen. "I picked out the house. But Trice decorated every room herself."

Charlene took a seat on the barstool in front of the island situated in the middle of the kitchen. After she sat down, she made a comment about it. "Oh my God! I've always wanted a kitchen like this. I love the fact that you got the stove built in the island. I'm so used to seeing kitchens with the stove placed by the wall."

"Yeah, me too. But it was all Trice's idea. She's very particular about what she likes and how she wants things to look."

"I could tell when I first laid eyes on her."

"Want something to drink?"

"You got beer?"

I opened the refrigerator and pulled out a bottle of wine. "Nope. But I got a bottle of Moscato."

Charlene smiled. "That's even better."

I popped the bottle open and poured us a glass of wine. But before we took the first sip, Charlene raised her glass in the air and suggested we make a toast. "To the future," she said.

"To the future," I repeated, and then we clinked wineglasses.

We both put the glasses up to our lips simultaneously and allowed the flow of the wine to pour into our mouths. It was cold and sweet, harmony to my taste buds.

I could tell Charlene liked it too. Amazingly, it took her a matter of sixty seconds to swallow the entire glass. Immediately after she set the glass down before her, she let out a loud and disgusting burp and then she smiled. "Now that was really good."

"Sounds like you've got indigestion."

She smiled bashfully and covered her mouth. "I guess you're right."

I picked up the bottle of Moscato and poured

her another glass. "Take your time, sweetheart. There's a lot more where this came from," I told her.

She took a sip and then she said, "I know. But it's so good."

I walked back over to the refrigerator and grabbed a block of cheddar cheese. Then I grabbed a pack of Ritz crackers from the bread container. "Got some cheese and crackers," I announced as I set the items down in front of Charlene.

"I've never had cheese and crackers with wine before," she acknowledged.

"You've got to be kidding me, right?" I replied as I grabbed a cheese knife from the utensil drawer.

"Trust me, I'm dead serious. Me and Leon is that ghetto couple you'll see hanging out at the local bootleg spot taking shots until we fall out. But when we're at home, we'll sip on alcohol with a bag of chips or a bowl of peanuts in our hands."

"That's not ghetto. Hell, I used to get it cracking the same way. My wife, Trice, got me on the wine with the cheese and cracker thing. She's a high-maintenance type with an image. So when it's time to entertain her family and friends, she pulls out the most expensive wine or champagne and then she'll prepare them a cheese, vegetable, and fruit plate. And everyone loves it."

"So you're married to one of those high-class types, huh?"

"Something like that," I commented as I began to cut up the cheese and make little bite-size sandwiches.

"How long y'all been married?"

"Seven years," I told her, and then I bit down on the cracker with the piece of cheese.

"How long were y'all together before you got married?" she asked, and then she bit down into the cheese with the cracker.

"Three years."

"How old is she?"

"Trice is thirty-five. She got me by two years."

"Oh, so you're a young buck, huh?"

"How old are you?" I asked her.

"Twenty-seven," she replied bashfully.

"You're the young buck!" I commented jokingly.

Charlene burst into laughter. She must've found my comment to be amusing. So while she smiled, I got a chance to get a good look at her teeth. And I had to admit that they were beautiful. Judging from her mannerisms, she was a street chick. But I could see that there was a softer side buried beneath her hard shell. I've heard a lot of stories from Leon about how lazy Charlene was and how she hardly ever cooked. He even complained about how she nagged all the fucking time. But there was nothing unusual about that. All women nagged if they weren't getting their way. It's just what women were born to do.

So while I was staring at her, she broke my train of thought by asking me what was I staring at. Without hesitation, I told her the truth. She looked as if she were at a loss for words. And instead of making a comment, she looked at me in a provocative way. A few seconds later, she licked her lips in a manner in which she was inviting me to shove my tongue down her throat. Her actions completely caught me off guard. But I played it off and remained cool about it. I even went to the extent of acting like what she did never happened.

I also changed the subject as I looked down at my watch. "Damn, time is flying. I gotta make a quick call," I lied. And while I began to walk away from her, I assured her I would be right back.

As soon as I stepped out of the kitchen and into the hallway, my urge to rip her panties off and fuck the shit out of her diminished a little bit. My dick was hard as a rock, but it slowly deflated in size as I walked farther away from her. And to make sure I got myself back on track, I rushed outside to the back patio to get some fresh air. I guessed I must've stayed gone too long because I heard her calling my name.

When I reentered the house, she was standing

in the hallway. "Do you mind if I take a shower?" she asked me.

"Nah, go ahead," I told her as I continued toward her.

She stood there in a skimpy-looking sundress. I was shocked that Leon allowed her to leave the house like that. I could literally see through the damn thing. She left nothing to the imagination. I could tell from five feet away how thick her thighs were and how tiny her waist was. She was sexy as hell. She wasn't as pretty as Trice, but she was thicker. She was basically any man's dream sex toy. And if her fuck game was anything like her body, she'd definitely be a prize.

"Where do you keep your towels?" she asked me, and then she put her right hand on her hip.

"Upstairs in the hallway linen closet next to the bathroom."

She smiled at me and said, "Thanks." Immediately thereafter she turned her back to me and headed upstairs.

I couldn't help but watch her as she walked away. Her ass was so fat that my dick got hard all over again. If she would've stripped down and got butt naked right there in front of me, I know I would've jumped dead on her and not feel a thing for her after I busted my nut. Shit, men did it all the time. So maybe before all this was over, I would have my chance. I just hoped that she was one of those chicks who didn't catch feelings. I couldn't afford for her to get attached to me, because it wouldn't be a good look. More importantly, Trice wouldn't be too happy about that. And I was sure Leon wouldn't be happy about it either.

Meanwhile, while Charlene showered, I started cleaning up around the kitchen. As I was putting everything away, I heard her cell phone ring. I picked it up off the island where she had set it and looked down at the caller ID. When I noticed it was Leon calling her, I rushed upstairs to hand her the phone. I knocked on the door when I approached the bathroom.

"It's open," she yelled.

I cracked the door open just enough to stick my arm inside. "Leon is calling you," I told her.

"Tell 'im I'm in the shower and I'll call him back," she instructed me.

"Come on, Charlene, you know better than that! How do you think that's gon' look with me answering your phone? Nah, you tell him," I replied as I stretched my arm out farther so she'd be able to grab her phone.

But before she could grab and answer it, the phone stopped ringing. While I stood there with the phone in my hand, I heard her turn off the shower and step out of the tub. I couldn't see what she was doing, but I felt her vibration on the floor as she walked toward my arm. With her wet hands, she finally took her phone from me;

then she opened the bathroom door so I could get a full view of her body. I couldn't help it, but my dick rose to its fullest peak. The jean shorts I had on didn't help to conceal my manhood at all.

When Charlene noticed it, she smiled and said, "Well, it didn't take long to get you aroused."

Making sure my back was to the cameras, I placed my hands over the bulge in my shorts and smiled bashfully. "That's because I see something I like," I finally said as I looked at her from head to toe.

Indeed she was about ten to fifteen pounds thicker than Trice, but Charlene's body was eye candy. Her titties weren't perky, but they didn't sag either. I guessed they had to be a C cup because they looked like they could fit in the palm of my hands easily. Her tummy was as flat as a board. It was hard to tell she had had a child because I didn't see a stretch mark anywhere. And as my eyes moved down to her camel toe, I noticed she had a gap between her inner thighs, which I thought was sexy as hell. I love to see chicks with a fat butt and thick thighs with that gap between the upper parts of their thighs. That shit made me wild and crazy.

I did notice a few spots of cellulite in her hip areas. But it wasn't enough to talk about. She'd had a baby, so she got a pass in my book. I just hoped she'd let me test the waters and keep her mouth closed after the fact. Can't have my homeboy putting out a hit on my life especially behind a piece of pussy.

While her body was dripping with water, she placed her left hand on her hip and said, "Well, if you like it, then why are you just standing there?"

I stood there with the dumbest-looking expression on my face. Although she'd just invited me to come and test the water, I instantly got cold feet. I mean, I didn't know this chick for real. All I knew about her was that she was my homeboy's wife and in less than two hours, she had made my dick hard twice. So she could be trying to set me up. Cry rape if I bend her ass over and fuck the shit out of her. And I wasn't trying to have that. I didn't need that headache. With a rape charge came attorney's fees for a divorce, prison time, and a big old sex offender label stuck on my forehead. And since it wasn't a smart move to acquire any of these things, I shook my head and took two steps backward.

Charlene gave me a disappointed look. "Where are you going? I thought you like what you saw?" she questioned me.

"I do. But I got too much to lose. Plus, I don't need the drama," I told her.

She leaned toward me, but didn't cross the threshold of the bathroom. "I promise, I won't cause you any drama. No one will ever hear about this. This will be our little secret," she replied, seductively beckoning me into the bathroom. Hoping my actions didn't look suspicious on the camera, I stepped inside the bathroom. Immediately, she pressed her naked body against mine and wrapped her arms around me. The feeling of her pussy pressed against my dick sent an electric shock through my groin that shot directly to my heart. I swear I immediately wanted to rip my own fucking clothes off, but I played it cool. I didn't want to seem too eager. But my plans went straight out of the window, because as soon as she released her arms from around my neck, she turned her body completely around and pressed her fat ass against my dick.

And when I say my dick was pulsating, believe me, that's an understatement. I felt like a fucking teenager getting my first piece of pussy on prom night. My adrenaline was pumping like mad and all the worries of the consequences I could face went out the window. I wanted to fuck her! Point-blank! And if she'd promise to keep her damn mouth closed, I'd give her the best piece of dick she would ever have in her life.

While a whole bunch of shit was going through my mind, she pressed her ass against my dick a tad bit harder. Then she grabbed my hands and placed them on her breasts. I took the lead and began to massage them while I ground my dick into her soft, fat ass. She loved what I was doing to her more than I was enjoying it, because she started talking really reckless.

She reminded me of a whore in a porno movie. "I want you to fuck me hard!" she began. "I want you to shove your dick deep in my pussy! And then I want you to fuck me in my ass!"

I was caught off guard by all the shit she was talking. But did I mention that I liked every damn word she uttered from her mouth? It'd been a long time since I fucked around on my wife. And with the chicks I used to fuck around with, they never talked to me like this. Hell, it had been prior to my marriage since a chick had talked like this to me and I had to admit, this turned me on.

Come to think about it, I believed that if my wife would sometimes act hood and gutter like this, then our sex life would be much better. See, Trice liked the regular missionary position. Plus, she wasn't into sucking my dick, so my sex life was pretty much ordinary. Actually, it sucked. Believe me, I probably would've left her a long time ago if I were only in the relationship for the sex. Thank God she's smart and she could cook a damn good decent meal. If it wasn't for that, I would've bailed out on her a long time ago and got with someone like this butt-naked chick bent over in front of me.

"Troy, please stop making me wait!" Charlene

started whining. "I want to feel your big dick inside of me," she begged.

"I wanna push my dick inside of you too," I assured her as I grabbed a hold of her hips and pulled her closer to me as I ground on her ass harder.

"Fuck me now!" she continued to beg. So I unzipped my jean shorts and pulled my dick out through the slit of my boxer shorts. My meat was hard as a rock and it had started dripping right before my eyes. I couldn't wait any longer, so I grabbed her hips to cock up her ass so it would be easy for me to slide my dick inside of her pussy. While I was trying to find her hole, it dawned on me that I needed a condom. I couldn't fuck her without protection. I wasn't trying to get this broad pregnant, nor was I trying to catch something. Trice would fucking kill me if I brought her back a case of herpes or worse. So I stopped in my tracks and said, "Wait, I need a condom."

She sucked her teeth. "Hurry up and get one because my pussy is hot and it is throbbing for you," she replied as she looked back at me.

I immediately became devastated because I didn't have any condoms. Trice and I had been together for over seven years and the last time I fucked around on her was about three years ago. So if I did have any condoms, they would be expired by now, which meant I was up a creek without a paddle. What the hell was I going to do? My dick was rock hard and I had a butt-naked, big-booty chick in my grasp and I hadn't the slightest idea how I was going to maneuver this situation.

I was fighting with the decisions of fucking her without a condom and risk getting something I couldn't get rid of or getting her pregnant. Damn, what was a man to do?

Charlene stood straight up and turned toward me. She wrapped her arms around my neck and began to kiss me on the lips. "Come on, Troy, whatcha gon' do? Let this good pussy go to waste?" she uttered between kisses.

She was making it really hard for me to turn her down. But I knew I had to stand for something. Because like I said, I had a lot to lose. In other words, I couldn't let a piece of pussy ruin that for me. I had willpower. So that's what I intended to use.

"As bad as I wanna fuck you, Charlene, I can't go there, baby girl," I finally told her, and then I gently pushed her away from me.

She didn't take me seriously because she forced herself on me. But as soon as she pulled me into her arms, I pushed her back with a little force. This time when I got her off me, I turned around and left her standing where she stood. I thought she was going to run behind and pursue me more, but she didn't. I was glad. If she had, I don't think I would've been able to resist her any longer. Plus, she would get caught naked on camera. God knew what he was doing. I wasn't a religious type of cat, but I remember growing up and hearing my mama say that God wouldn't put more on me than I could bear. So I take those words everywhere I go, whether it be a good situation or bad. Who knew what would've happened if I'd given her the dick? I could see Leon shooting me in the fucking head if he knew I chopped his wife down. Fucking another man's woman wasn't something men took lightly. Men are like dogs. We mark our territory and dare niggas to cross that line. Fucking another man's woman was also a pride issue. You can't fuck with a man's woman and expect him not to hurt you if his feelings are invested. Niggas take heartbreaks worse than women. We play the tough role, but when the shit hits the fan, we lose our damn minds. In short, niggas are softer than chicks when it comes to falling in love. But we'd never admit it.

I found myself getting away from Charlene and went into the nearest bathroom. With all the action Charlene laid on me, I had to release the beast. There was no way I'd be able to go to bed with the monkey I had on my back. I had this huge buildup and I was going to get it out of me. I grabbed the bottle of baby oil from the medicine cabinet and then I handled my business. *There's nothing like safe sex!*

3

Trice

"What are you doing?" I asked Troy the moment he answered the phone.

"Straightening things up around the kitchen. Why?" he asked me.

I ignored his question because I had a few more of my own. "You sure you're in the kitchen? Because it doesn't sound like it."

"How is it supposed to sound?" he asked.

Again, I ignored his question and asked him one more of my own. "Where is Charlene?"

"She's upstairs. Why?"

"Because Leon just tried to call her, and she didn't answer her cell phone."

"That's because her phone is down here in the kitchen."

"What is she doing upstairs?" I wanted to know. Shit, the bitch could have been upstairs in my bedroom snooping through my personal belongings and I couldn't have that.

"She asked me where the bathroom was, so I believe she's up there taking a shit or something," he replied in a joking manner.

I wasn't feeling his jokes, so I quickly put him in check. "Troy, please don't get cute right now. I am not in the damn mood. All I asked is what you were doing and then I asked you what she was doing, because her husband just tried to get in touch with her. So don't act like this shit is all fun and games."

"Look, Trice, I am not acting like anything. Right now I am trying to get the kitchen straight, because I know how you are about dishes being dirty overnight. So—"

I cut him off in midsentence. "What dishes are you talking about? I cleaned up the kitchen before I left the house."

"Well, I pulled out some leftovers from the refrigerator and microwaved them. So I had a few items that were dirty."

"Troy, you better not be lying to me," I said sternly. I could tell when he was lying to me. He had done it plenty of times in the past, especially when I suspected that he'd cheated on me with an attorney named Lisa Alvarez. To this day he denies ever sleeping with her, but I saw the text messages. The writing was on the wall, even though I didn't actually catch him in the act. And if he knew like I knew, he'd better not get caught out there again or it's bon voyage.

"Listen, baby, I am not lying to you. So don't start getting paranoid on me. Believe me, I am not going to do anything that would jeopardize my marriage. I don't give a damn who she is or how much money she has. You are my wife and I won't let anyone come between us. You follow me?"

I hesitated for a bit and then I responded. "Yes, I follow you."

"All right. Well, let me get back to what I was doing. And I'll call you back before I go to bed."

I sighed heavily. "Okay," I replied.

"I love you," he told me.

"I love you too," I assured him.

Immediately after I hung up with Troy, I went back into the den area and joined Leon. He was once again engrossed in another episode of *Two and a Half Men*. He was laughing his butt off too. I took a seat beside him and forced myself to watch the show. I figured it would take my mind off my temporary living arrangements. But that idea went straight out the window, because as soon as a commercial came on, Leon focused on me.

"Did you get a chance to talk to Troy?" he asked me.

"Yeah, I just hung up with him."

"Did you get a chance to tell him I tried to call Charlene?"

"Yeah, I told him. And he said she was upstairs using our bathroom," I responded nonchalantly, and then gazed back at the TV.

"You all right?"

"Yeah, I'm fine," I assured him without looking at him.

"Well, you look like you're on the verge of crying."

"No, I'm not about to cry. I'm just a little frustrated is all."

"Care to talk about it?" he pressed the issue.

I shook my head and told him no. I also told him that it really wasn't important and I was just going through the motions. "I'll be fine by the morning," I continued.

Leon shrugged and said, "Okay."

After the sitcom ended, I retired to Leon's son's bedroom. I laid in the dark for almost two hours waiting for Troy to call me back. By the time ten o'clock rolled around, my cell phone still had not rung. I was furious and took it upon myself to call him, since it seemed as if he was too preoccupied to call me. Unfortunately for me, when I called his cell, he did not answer his phone. I called twice and allowed it to ring five times each call. Then I called the house phone and he managed to answer that line.

I ripped him a new asshole when he finally answered. "What the fuck is going on, Troy?" I snapped.

"What do you mean?"

"I just called your cell phone twice and you didn't answer it. So tell me what the hell you got going on that would prevent you from answering your damn phone?" I roared. I was pissed. The only thing that raced through my mind was the possibility of him fucking around with Leon's wife. And the thought of him doing it in my house got me sick to my stomach. What would be worse was if they were fooling around in my bed.

"Can you calm down for a minute and let me explain?" he snapped back.

"I'm listening."

"First off, I wasn't doing shit to prevent me from answering my phone. I'm chilling in our bedroom watching TV while my phone is charging up. So stop calling me with all the unnecessary drama. You giving me a fucking headache!"

When Troy screamed at me the way he did, I knew he was serious. And I could tell he wasn't doing anything he wasn't supposed to be doing. In the past when I suspected that he was doing underhanded shit, he'd stutter when I would ask him certain questions and he would sometimes avoid my questions altogether. So I felt like he was on his best behavior.

After he snapped at me, I fell silent because I

was at a loss for words. I really didn't know what to say because I was feeling really stupid. Thankfully enough, he broke the silence barrier and told me I had nothing to worry about. So after he assured me a couple more times that he wasn't thinking about Leon's wife, he gave me a kiss over the phone and told me good night. After I hung up the phone, I felt at ease and went straight to sleep.

The next morning I was awakened to some good-smelling breakfast food. It smelled like Leon was cooking a pan of turkey bacon and some pancakes. I wasn't a breakfast type of girl, but the way he had that kitchen smelling, I had to go downstairs to see what was going on. I slipped on my robe, went into the bathroom to freshen up, and then I headed downstairs. I had my hair wrapped with a couple of bobby pins, so I looked somewhat presentable.

"Good morning," I said as I entered the kitchen.

Leon's back was to me when I walked in, so I startled him. He jumped just a tad and then turned around completely. "I am so sorry for startling you," I told him.

"You're cool," he replied, and then he turned his attention back to the pan and the cooking utensil he had in his hand.

I took a seat in one of the chairs placed around

the kitchen table. "Do I smell turkey bacon and pancakes?"

"You sure do. You hungry?"

"I normally don't eat breakfast, but you got it smelling really good in here."

Leon stacked two pancakes on a plate and then placed three slices of turkey bacon on top of the pancakes. "After you sink your teeth into this, you ain't gonna look at breakfast food in a negative manner ever again," he stated, and then he walked over and set the plate directly in front of me.

"Yeah. Yeah. Yeah," I commented, and then I smiled. It's really funny because even though Leon wasn't my type of man, he was very charismatic. The more I hung around him the more I noticed he was developing something I never thought he had—sex appeal. He stood before me shirtless, so I was able to get a full view of his washboard abs and enormous pecs and biceps. It took everything within me not to comment on his body. I felt like it wouldn't be appropriate considering he was my husband's friend.

The butter he placed on top of my pancakes melted instantly, so he took the liberty to assist me by pouring a hefty amount of syrup onto my plate. "Taste it and tell me if you like it," he encouraged me.

I grabbed the fork that was placed before me

and cut into the pancakes. The syrup and butter soaked heavily into the pancakes and made them look delicious. When I shoved the first bite of pancakes into my mouth, my taste buds went haywire. The pancakes damn near melted in my mouth.

Leon noticed how I was enjoying his work of art, so he made it his business to comment on it. "I told you it was good, didn't I?"

I smiled with a mouthful of food and gave him a nod.

He grabbed himself a plate of pancakes and a few strips of bacon. Then he took a seat at the table across from me. He tore into his food as if there were no tomorrow. I sat there and watched him eat every single morsel of food. His table etiquette was on zero, but his cooking skills were charted at ten on the scale. It took me longer to finish my food. And when I was done, Leon politely took my plate and started cleaning the kitchen. Meanwhile, he and I got into a heavy conversation while I continued to sit at the table.

"Talk to Troy this morning?" he asked as he paraded around the kitchen in his blue Nike basketball shorts and bedroom slippers.

"Yeah, I talked to him before he went off to work."

"I thought he was off today."

"He was but he got a call early this morning telling him he had to come in."

"That's crazy that they make him work damn near six days a week."

"I know. He hates it. But what can he do when there are bills to pay?"

"Yeah. True. But those crackers 'round there don't give niggas like me and Troy no slack. They're quick to call us to come in and work six days a week, but they bite their damn tongues when it's time to give out raises, which is why I bailed out on their asses and got me a job at the Nissan dealership in Chesapeake. Those people over there take care of their employees, which is why you see me walking around in my kitchen right now. I keep telling Troy to come over there with me, but he won't listen to me."

"It's not like he doesn't want to come. It's just that he's been with Lexus for so long, he doesn't want to lose his seniority and his benefits."

"Excuse my French, Trice, but fuck them damn benefits they dishing out. That shit they trying to pass off to us is bogus as hell. Tell Troy to try using his vacation time and see how much trouble they give him. Them motherfuckers over there ain't shit. All they want to do is work you to death and send you home with a pat on the back. But no way, I got tired of them pimping me. So I jetted on their asses and I am doing better than ever now."

"Well, I don't believe Troy is having the problem you had. Because it seems like every time he calls in sick they don't give him a hard time."

Leon walked toward me and stopped. He wanted me to give him my undivided attention and that's exactly what I did. "See, them crackers over there don't give a damn about sick leave. But they do care about that vacation time and the raises. So when Troy starts to ask for one of them, then trust me, they're going to give him some problems. Mark my words."

I sat there and listened to the words Leon uttered from his mouth. But I was more focused on his physique. I was completely mesmerized. I also couldn't help but notice how big his dick was. It hung from his groin area like a horse penis. It easily rested on the middle of his thigh. I wanted to ask him if he'd ever measured it, but I knew that would be crass and dead wrong if I spoke those words. Not only would I be disrespecting Troy, but I would be disrespecting myself as well. So I casually moved my gaze away from his private area and focused on his face. Besides, he was talking to me. So I did the right thing, the polite thing, and focused on his face.

Once he got all the mayhem he experienced working for the Lexus dealership off his chest, he asked about my and Troy's plans to spend our ten thousand dollars.

I thought for a brief moment and then I said, "Well, I really don't want anything. Troy and I talked about him putting the money in our savings as an emergency fund. But I'm sure he's going to go out and buy me something nice. That's just his character."

It felt good explaining what I thought or hoped we would do with the money. I redirected the question to him. "So what have you and your wife decided to do with the money y'all will get?"

"Since I'm the breadwinner around here, I decided to pay off my truck. I only owe a little over eight grand. And then I'll probably use the rest on a set of new tires. If I got any left, I'll give Charlene a few bucks to get her hair done."

I burst into laughter. "All she gets is a hairstyle from the money?"

"You damn right! She better feel lucky if she gets that from me to get her hair done, especially when she gets her little disability checks and don't contribute any of it to the house fund. She's selfish as hell! All she thinks about is herself, which is why I was eager to get rid of her for the next seven days. And if you want to know the truth, I would've sent her ass off on a weeklong excursion even if those contest people weren't giving up the ten grand. That's just how bad I needed a break from her."

"Well, if y'all relationship is that bad, then why are you two together?"

Leon thought for a second and then he said, "It's my son that's keeping me here with her. If we didn't have him in our lives, then I would've left her years ago."

"What is it that you don't like about her? She seems like a nice girl. And besides, with all that ass she has, I know a few guys who would kill to have her."

"There are so many things I don't like about her. But the three things that stick out more to me is the fact that she's lazy, she doesn't like to cook, and she's a nagger. And as far as her ass is concerned, there's more to life than fucking a chick with a phat ass. I work my ass off for my family. So I need a woman who's a team player and my cheerleader. It wouldn't hurt to get a pat on my back every so often."

I burst into laughter once again. "Wow! I can't imagine her not doing that for you. She seems like she's Team Leon to me."

"Don't let her looks fool you."

"Well, don't give up on her so soon. Give her a chance. I'm sure she'll come around."

"I won't hold my breath."

"Have you two discussed the possibility of getting some marriage counseling?" I said.

"Who's gonna pay for it?" he shot back.

I threw my hands up as a defense shield.

"What! Hold up! Don't shoot the messenger," I commented, and then I cracked a smile.

Leon toned down his aggressive behavior and said, "I'm sorry, Trice. But if I gotta spend a coin to get someone to help me and Charlene to see eye-to-eye so we can stay together, then it's a moot issue for me, because it will never happen. I spend enough money to keep the household together. So to get me to spend money on something else is out of the question."

"Can you tell me what you like about her?" I asked him, in an effort to shift the conversation in a positive direction.

"Nope, I can't think of anything," he didn't hesitate to say.

"Come on, Leon, there has to be something other than the fact that she's the mother of your son."

He mulled over my question for a couple of seconds and then he broke his silence. "The sex is good. But that's about it."

I was appalled at his answer. But it also struck a chord with me because he'd just admitted that his wife was good in bed, which of course made me feel intimidated because this same woman was at my house entertaining my husband, who was a sex addict. One of the problems Troy and I had in our relationship was that he had a huge appetite for sex, whereas I only wanted to have it once a week. Not to mention, I didn't like to give him head. So I believed if Charlene was given a chance, then she might be able to woo him over.

The thought of how great she performed sexually got me sick to my stomach, so I immediately changed the subject. I got up from my chair and patted him on his shoulder. "Don't worry. It'll get better for you and her."

Leon chuckled at my statement. "Trust me, I ain't gonna hold my breath," he replied, and then he looked down at his wristwatch. "Time to go do my morning run."

"You work out?"

"Yep. I run at least two to three miles five days a week. I gotta keep my body in shape."

I gave him a puzzled look. "You didn't strike me as a man who worked out."

"What kind of man did you think I was?"

"Well, I knew you had 'locks on your head and that you hung out at the sports bar with Troy. So I automatically assumed you were a blunt-smoking Rasta who thought he was God's gift to women."

He smiled. "Really?"

"Yep."

"But I don't even smoke."

"I see that now."

"Wow! It's funny how people always make assumptions even when they only know a little about you."

"Very true," I agreed. "So where do you do your running?"

"I run around the track at Norfolk Academy. Why, you wanna go?"

"Sure. I would love to tag along. But wait, I don't think I packed anything I can work out in."

"Don't worry. I got a pair of gym shorts you could fit."

"All right. Well, let's do it," I replied as I waited for him to exit the kitchen so I could follow him to his bedroom to get the shorts he said I could borrow.

After he handed me the shorts, he told me to meet him downstairs by the front door when I had gotten dressed. I told him okay and disappeared into his son's bedroom.

When Leon and I got completely dressed for our morning run, we both hopped in his vehicle and then we headed to Norfolk Academy to use their track. En route to the track, Leon sparked up a conversation about my marriage to Troy. I was somewhat uncomfortable when he asked me the first few questions. I knew Troy and Leon had been friends for years, so in my mind, giving him the most intimate details of our relationship wasn't such a good idea. But when he assured me that whatever I told him would be safe and sound and that it wouldn't leave his vehicle, I became a little more relaxed.

"Have you ever gotten to a place in your relationship where you wanted to get a divorce?" he asked me.

I hesitated for a moment and then I said, "Yes, I have."

"Really? When?"

"When he cheated on me with this chick a few years back."

"Wow! I never heard about that."

"Oh yes, you did. I know he told you about her."

"I swear he didn't," Leon replied, and then he raised his right hand.

"Well, he cheated on me with Lisa Alvarez."

"You mean the bankruptcy lawyer who does those stupid, loud commercials on TV?"

"Yep, that's her."

"So, what prevented you from going through with the divorce?"

"I prayed about it and that's when God told me to give him another chance."

"You believe in that God stuff?"

"Of course I do."

"Do you go to church?"

"I used to."

"Why did you stop?"

"I have my reasons."

"Plan on going back?"

"Absolutely. But only after I find another church."

"Believe it or not, I tried going to church a few times."

"Really? You don't strike me as the type to attend church."

"And what type is that?"

"It's nothing really. Just tell me why you stopped going?"

"I got tired of giving away my money. Every time I turned around, the collection plate was being passed around. All the preachers want is to empty your pockets and send your ass home broke."

"Not all preachers are like that." I chuckled. Leon was a funny guy. With all the stories he had to tell, I knew I was going to go on the ride of my life.

4

Troy

When I woke up this morning, I had a hard-on that was out of this fucking world. And knowing that Charlene was in the next room didn't make my situation any easier. The thought of her grinding her ass up against my dick last night did something to me while I slept, because I couldn't get my mind off her. I just wished I could get a chance to taste her pussy without it backfiring on me. I mean, if I knew for sure that she would keep her mouth closed and Trice wouldn't find out about it, I would jump at the opportunity. There's nothing like fucking new pussy. The excitement and the rush that came from blowing a chick's back out was indescribable. I would say the wetter her pussy was the more enjoyable the sex. Too bad I walked away from the perfect opportunity to find out how wet her coochie got, because if it was anything like I imagined, then I would've been in for a treat.

So while I reminisced about our little episode last night, my BlackBerry rang. I looked at the caller ID and noticed it was Trice calling me back. When I spoke with her earlier, I told her I had to go in to work. I lied so she wouldn't be sweating me for most of the day by calling me all the time, wondering what Charlene and I were doing. Since she figured I was at work, I had to play the part. Unfortunately, there weren't enough acoustics in my bedroom to give off the sound that I was in a garage, so I grabbed my phone and raced downstairs and out the front door.

"Hello," I finally said, panting as if I was out of breath.

"Why you breathing so hard?" she asked me.

"That's because you called me while I was in the middle of carrying a shitload of car tires."

"What time are you getting off?"

"Probably around three. Why?"

"There's no particular reason. I just wanted to know."

"Well, what are you doing?"

"I just had breakfast and now I'm on my way out the door to take a morning run."

"Wait! When did you start running?"

"This morning. I figured it's time I start to get in shape."

"Who said you were out of shape?"

"Nobody. But what's wrong with building up my endurance?"

"Nothing at all."

"Exactly. So whatcha got planned after you get off work?"

"I don't have anything planned. Leon's wife did mention she wanted to rent a couple of movies from Redbox. But other than that, I have no real plans."

"So y'all are going to chill out and watch a couple of movies together, huh?" Trice replied. She sounded like she didn't like the idea of Charlene and me chilling. But hey, we were only gonna watch a couple of movies.

"Look, baby, I don't know why you're even sweating that. We're only gonna be sitting around in the den watching a movie and that's it. Nothing else. So, please don't stress yourself out about it."

"I'm not stressed out. But it amazes me that you can go out and rent movies for you two to watch, but if I asked you to do the same thing, you'd make up every excuse in the world about how busy you are or that you're not in the mood."

"You know what? You're right. But guess what?"

"What?"

"She and I got nothing else to do. But check it out, if you rather I take her out to dinner or take her to a movie, then I'll do that."

"Troy, don't be a smart-ass!" she snapped.

"I'm not being a smart-ass! I'm just trying to get you to see that what I am doing is harmless," I replied, and then I fell silent. I wanted to give her the opportunity to lay all the cards out on the table. But she didn't take the bait. She remained quiet, so I came back at her. "Look, Trice, I gotta go back to work. But in the meantime, don't stress yourself out. We only have six more days and then you're back at home. Not to mention, you'll be bringing home that ten-thousand-dollar check."

She sighed. "All right. Go back to work. But call me when you get off."

"I will," I assured her.

After I got off the phone with Trice, I felt bad knowing that I lied to her about being at work. But what else could I have done? I can't take her nagging all the fucking time. A man needs a break sometimes. And besides, there was nothing going on between Charlene and me. Granted,

I wanted to fuck her brains out, but I didn't. I used self-control because I had something better waiting to see me after this arrangement was over. I just wished Trice would see what was really on my heart concerning her.

5

Charlene

I slept like a baby last night even though I was in the bed alone. This was my second day at my husband's friend's house, and at the end of the seventh day Leon and I would be ten thousand dollars richer. My hands were itching as I thought about it. I swear I couldn't wait until we got that big check in our hands. It felt as if we're about to hit the damn lottery.

As I sat down on the bed in the guest room and thought about all the stuff I would get with the money, Troy knocked on the door. I was dressed appropriately in my blue satin pajama shorts with the shirt to match, but I felt as if I were overdressed and had to shed some clothing to see if I could entice Troy. So before I told him to come in, I took off my top and my bra and then I told him to enter. When he turned the doorknob to open the door, I acted as if I was trying to put on my bra. He caught another glimpse of my C cups. But he quickly stepped back out the door and covered his eyes with his hand.

"I'm sorry. I thought you were dressed," he said.

"It's okay. You can come in," I told him.

He pulled the door back but left a slight crack open so he'd be able to communicate with me. I couldn't see his face, but I could hear him pretty well.

"Nah, I'm cool. I was on my way out to the store and wanted to know if you wanted me to pick you up something while I was there?"

I thought for a second. "Yeah, pick up a pack of condoms," I replied.

He hesitated a minute. I knew I caught him off guard with my response. I laughed to myself and approached the bedroom door with my bra and shirt in hand. When I grabbed a hold of the doorknob, Troy let it go and stood there.

I smiled at him and took another step toward him. "So are you going to get me the condoms or not?"

He didn't respond. Instead, he looked back at both cameras that were installed on both ends of the hallway. "You're afraid that your wife is going to see me naked on tape, huh?"

"Yeah, so you need to get back inside the room."

"Don't worry because I've already disconnected the wires in both cameras."

Troy became alarmed. "But why did you do that? The technicians told us not to tamper with the cameras or we'd forfeit the money."

"Stop sweating it. I can rig it back up."

"Well, do it. Because my wife would kill me if I lost that money."

I smiled at him and very casually began to put my bra and shirt back on as he turned to leave. It was a misleading smile. I started to tell him to go straight to hell. But I decided against it and closed the bedroom door. I mean, who did he think he was? I've never had a man turn me down in all the years I had been fucking. I was a bad bitch with some good pussy, a top contender when it came to sucking dick, and I liked to get fucked in my ass.

So what was his fucking problem?

He had to be gay or something because this just didn't happen to me. Not only that, but also his fucking wife was an average chick who volunteered her time to homeless shelters and whatnots. I wasn't your typical ride-or-die chick. I was the type that would go harder, and he needed to recognize that before it was too late.

And whether he knew it or not, I hated to be turned down. So I vowed I would get him to fuck me before I left this house. I already had it in my mind that when I was done with him, he was gonna wish he'd given me the dick the first night I walked through his front door. You could mark my words on that.

After he left the house, I pulled out my phone and called Leon, my husband. It was a nice Saturday morning, so I knew he'd either be out running or he'd be just getting back in the house and on his way to take a shower. But to my surprise, he didn't answer, which was kind of odd. Leon always carried his cell phone everywhere he went, so why wasn't he answering my call now?

Pissed off by his actions, I hung up the phone and threw it on the bed. Then the thought of what he could be doing with Troy's wife quickly followed. She wasn't all that pretty to me but I knew she was Leon's type. He used to always tell me how I needed to act more like a lady than a 'hood chick. But I wasn't about to let him tell me how to live. Shit, he met me while I was living in the 'hood with my mama, so what did he expect me to do? Act like I'm some bougie chick from Virginia Beach or something? Hell nah!

I was one of those chicks that would go out on the block and flip a couple of packages, or shake my ass at a strip club if I had to, so he needed to be grateful before I left his ass and got with a man who would appreciate me. And whether Troy believed it or not, he might just be that man.

While he was at the store, I rearranged the wires on both of the cameras in the hallway to make it look as if I fixed them. I knew he'd probably go behind me and check them. This was my shell game. I refused to reconnect them because I didn't want the cameras to catch any footage of me trying to seduce Troy. I also couldn't risk the people getting any footage of me going into their bedroom. So, while I had time, I snuck into their room and started rummaging through their things.

I couldn't care less about Troy's things. Trice's things were what I was interested in. I wanted to see what type of perfume she wore and I wanted to see how tidy she kept her closet. When I looked at her cosmetics on her vanity, I quickly learned that she was a Prada and a Givenchy girl when it came to the smell goods. Additionally, when I looked in her closet, I could tell she had a shoe fetish out of this world. She didn't have all the name-brand shoes like all the celebrities I saw on TV, but she had a big collection of Nine West, Bebe, and Nicole Miller. Her shoe size was an eight. I was a nine, so trying on her shoes to see how they looked on my feet was out of the question.

After I looked through her shoes, I looked at every shirt, skirt, and dress she had hanging up in her closet. To my surprise, Troy had more clothes than Trice. His clothes took up the most space in the closet. Of course, that was a complete turn-on for me. The labels in his clothes were Ralph Lauren, Lacoste, True Religion, and Rock & Republic. His cologne collection consisted of Unforgivable by Sean John, Ed Hardy, Gucci, and Burberry. The one that stood out for me was the Burberry, and I was gonna make sure I made him aware of that.

While I was going through Trice's panty drawers to see if she had any panties with holes in it or stains in the crotch area, I heard Troy unlocking the front door. Thoughts of him catching me looking at his and his wife's personal shit made my heart race, so I quietly closed her top drawer and slipped back out of their bedroom before he could step foot into the foyer of the house. He called my name right after he closed and locked the front door.

I stood at the top of the stairs and answered him. "Yes."

"I stopped by Denny's and got you and me some breakfast," he yelled from the kitchen.

"Okay, I'll be down there in a minute," I told him, and then I raced back to his bedroom to see if I left anything out of place. I refused to leave any evidence that would let him know I had been in his room, much less going through his things. When I was done, I made my way downstairs to join him in the kitchen.

When I entered the kitchen, he had my food laid out on the kitchen table with a tall glass of orange juice. I didn't know whether to thank him or pretend he wasn't in the room, since he'd chewed me out before he left the house. I wasn't expecting him to say anything to me about it, but he did. It shocked the hell out of me.

He stood with his back against the stove and gave me the sincerest look he could give me. "I'm sorry about earlier," he said.

I took a seat at the table. "It's okay. Don't worry about it," I assured him. I was really trying to smooth things over and make him think everything was cool between us. Then I was going to come back on him like a thief in the night. I had to admit I was jealous of the fact that Troy loved his wife. And the fact that he resisted all this ass I had because he didn't want to cheat on her made me even more jealous.

I could use all my fingers and toes and count the number of times Leon had cheated on me. So to run into a man who didn't cheat made me a bit envious.

Why can't I have a man like Troy? Why did I have to have Leon as my fucking husband?

All the shit Troy said Trice did for him, I used to do. I used to iron all his clothes, keep the laundry washed, and stayed in the kitchen, cooking my ass off. But as soon as Leon started cheating on me, I stopped it all. Cold turkey like a muthafucka. I wasn't about to be his fucking maid and slave, cooking his ass hot meals while he was out fucking different hoes. No way!

When I got my chance to fuck around on him, I did it. But what I hadn't done was fuck one of his homeboys. I knew that would upset his perfect little world. And before I leave this household, I was gonna have another secret to write down in my diary.

Once Troy was done with his apology, I dug into my food and he joined me. We ate and talked about my son. About how I knew I was going to miss him for the summer. Then we talked about the NBA play-offs. He got excited that I loved basketball, because his wife didn't. That was one thing he and I had in common. He ate that idea up.

That was my cue to pour the syrup on thick. Before he even realized it, I had him eating out of my hands once again. I figured out very quickly that I couldn't be the aggressor. I had to do some sneaky shit behind his back if I wanted to seduce him. So I put my thinking cap on and started coming up with a better plan.

First I started acting like I was really into sports. Niggas loved when they found a chick who loved or had the same hobbies at them.

He'd look at you like one of the boys but with the feminine features of a woman. Men loved to eat and drink while watching the game too. So I figured that if I whipped up a batch of finger foods and had a couple of cold beers at his disposal I'd earn all the brownie points. Second, men hated when chicks whined or complained about everything underneath the sun, so if I agreed with everything he uttered from his lips, I'd be on his good side for sure. Cats always wanted to be right, even when they knew that they were wrong. So, I knew that if I put my best foot forward and front like I was down for him, he'd lower his guard and come to me with open arms. I figured if all went well, I'd have him begging for this pussy in a matter of twenty-four to forty-eight hours.

Ain't nothing like manipulation. It was a girl's best friend.

6

Leon

This was the first time I'd ever had someone tag along with me while I did my morning run. It was really nice to have such a sexy woman run by my side and go as hard as Trice did. She turned me on like a muthafucka. So when we got back to my house, I thanked her for hanging out with me. She climbed up the stairs to get to the front door as if she was out of breath.

"You're welcome. But warn me the next time you want to run more than three miles. My legs aren't used to that much exercise at once," she told me as she stood by the front door and waited for me to open it.

"Don't you feel good, though?" I asked her.

She exhaled. "I guess."

I opened the front door and allowed her to go ahead of me. She was sweating bullets. But she looked good doing it. "I gotta jump in the shower right now," she insisted.

"Be my guest," I replied, and watched her as she walked away from me. She headed upstairs and I got an eyeful. Seeing women sweat from working out was the sexiest thing in the world. If I could get my wife to work out with me, then our marriage would probably turn around in a ninety-degree angle.

After Trice disappeared into the bathroom, I headed to the bathroom in my bedroom so I could get out of my sweaty clothes as well.

My cell phone rang as I began undressing. I knew it was Charlene, so I answered it without looking at the caller ID. "Hello."

"Where you been at?" she roared through the phone. She sounded very angry.

"I went running. Why?" I snapped back. I wasn't in the mood to argue with her. She always brought out the worst in me. With the good morning I was having with Trice, I definitely wasn't about to let her ruin it. She was a fucking drama queen. Hell, if I decided to hang up on her, I damn sure wouldn't have lost any sleep behind it.

"I called you earlier, but you didn't answer your phone. So I wanted to know where you been!" she continued to roar. But I let what she said go in one ear and out the other.

"Look, Charlene, if you called me to fuss, then I'm gonna hang up, because I'm not gonna let you give me a headache this morning."

"Leon, I know you ain't trying to show off in front of Troy's wife. You know I don't play that shit! I will hop in a cab and come right over there and blow up your spot. So you better change your fucking tone!"

I knew what she said was in fact true because that's the type of game she plays. That was how she rolled. She loved to draw attention to herself and make me look bad in the process. But I was not about to feed into her bullshit. So before she said another word, I politely told her I would call her back after I got out of the shower and then I pressed the END button on my phone. I knew she would try to call me back, so I turned my phone off immediately after I hung up on her. We didn't have a house phone, so I didn't have to worry about her calling it.

It didn't take me long to shit, shower, and shave. I was in and out of the bathroom in thirty minutes flat. I heard Trice rummaging around in my son's bedroom when I walked into the hallway. I knocked on the door. "Wanna go hang out?" I yelled through the door.

She opened the door to answer me. "Sure. Where you wanna go?"

I was getting ready to ask if she wanted to go

see a movie, but I was sidetracked by the smell of her perfume and the way she looked in her sundress. The dress wasn't all that glamorous, but it had sex appeal. To see her hair combed back into a ponytail was also sexy. She had on a pair of diamond-studded earrings and a diamond-encrusted pendant hung around her neck. She looked like the girl next door. And when she smiled, it took my breath away.

"Where do you wanna go?" she asked me once again.

I had to be honest and let down my guard. "You got a brother speechless right now," I admitted.

She smiled at me again. But this time it was one of those bashful type of smiles. "I wish my husband would talk to me like that," she told me.

"Wait, you telling me Troy doesn't tell you how beautiful you are?" I asked her.

She walked out of the bedroom and into the hall. "No. He doesn't."

I let her walk in front of me so I could get a better look at her. Her ass wasn't as fat as Charlene's, but it was nice. The idea of spanking her ass while I bent her over gave me chills. I knew I was wrong for thinking about my homeboy's wife, but I couldn't stop being a man. I was sure Troy was looking at my wife the same way. And the only difference with the way I felt about my wife versus him was that I couldn't care less if he fucked Charlene. That's just how I felt about the whole thing.

Chicks like my wife came a dime a dozen. But to have a woman like Trice was like winning the lottery. And the chances of getting a chick like Trice on your team was like one in a million. Since I knew it would be a long shot that I would ever hook up with someone like her, I figured there wasn't anything wrong with me relishing in the moment while I had her.

"I know you probably hear this all the time, but if you were my wife, I would be with you every chance I got. I mean, you are so pretty and down to earth. You're not flashy or arrogant. And I like the fact that you were willing to go running with me this morning. The thought of you taking care of your body is a huge thing for me."

She didn't respond to my comments, but she did smile.

When we got downstairs, I finally remembered to ask her if she wanted to go check out a movie.

"Yes, I would love to go to the movies," she replied cheerfully.

"Well, let's go, then," I said, and led her out of the house. I rushed toward the passenger side door of my white Dodge Magnum. As soon as she stepped to the curb, I opened the door for her and after she got in, I closed it.

She smiled the entire time. I knew I was winning brownie points with her. That was just the way I wanted it. She was a beautiful woman. And I was so happy to have her in my company.

Immediately after I got inside the car, I wondered why a beautiful woman like her didn't have any children. She seemed totally taken aback when I put the question to her, but she still answered.

"Troy and I have tried a couple times, but so far nothing has happened."

"Have y'all tried that in vitro shit? I heard that shit works."

"Yes, and it cost an arm and a leg too."

"Maybe you two should use the money from this show."

"I thought about it. But I don't think Troy is going to be down with that. He's a practical guy, so I'm sure he's gonna wanna continue to do it the traditional way."

"If you were my wife, I'd do anything you want." I assured her. Trice was a sweetheart in my eyes. Too bad she belonged to my homeboy.

She smiled. "Yeah, right. Tell me anything."

"I wanna tell you something else, but with respect to my boy Troy, I'm gonna be on my best behavior."

"Yeah, you do that," she replied, and then she smiled once again.

The way she smiled at me gave me a glimmer of hope that I may be able to crack that lock Troy had on her.

Patience is the key.

7

Troy

Charlene stepped out of the TV room when she got Leon on the phone. She went into the kitchen to get a little privacy, but I still heard her fussing with Leon. A minute or two into their conversation, I heard her mumble underneath her breath about how he had hung up on her in an earlier conversation. Boy, was she angry. Instead of coming back into the TV room with me, she went outside. I peeped through the mini-blinds of my living room window and saw her pacing back and forth on the front lawn area with her arms folded. From where I was standing, I could tell that she was talking to herself. That was a bad sign. When women did that, niggas had to watch out. *A woman scorned is a treacherous woman who will pour sugar in your gas tank and then laugh in your face.* That's what my dad used to tell me. I thank God I wasn't on her shit list.

When I got tired of staring at her from the window, I exited the front room of the house and made my way back to the TV room. There was a Victoria's Secret commercial on TV that reminded me of Trice and that prompted me to call her. I knew my surroundings needed to sound like I was at work, so I turned the volume of the TV down. I prayed Charlene would stay outside while I was on the phone, because I didn't need her blowing my cover.

Come to find out, it really didn't matter because Trice didn't answer her phone. I called her three times back-to-back, and each time it rang four times and went to voice mail. I didn't normally do this, but I called Leon's phone to get him to relay the message for her to answer her phone. Hell, his phone didn't ring at all. It went straight to voice mail. That was unusual for Leon's phone to be off. I had never called his phone and had it go straight to voice mail. So my gut instinct told me something wasn't right with this picture. However, before I drew a conclusion, I tried calling her two more times. Again, it rang four times and then went to voice mail.

I had to admit that I wasn't happy about my wife not answering her phone. I couldn't say what she had going on that prevented her from answering her phone, but whatever it was it couldn't be that important.

Several minutes later, Charlene came back into the house. She walked straight back to where I was. She didn't make it a secret that she was upset. She slumped down on the sofa next to me and ranted like she was upset with the entire world.

"I swear, I can't wait until this week is over because after those people give me and him that check, I'm gonna get my half off the top and then I'm leaving his sorry ass!"

I started to probe into her business, because I knew Leon did something to upset her to the point she thought about divorcing him. My curiosity was killing me. I figured that whatever it was, maybe it had something to do with Trice. But strange things tend to happen and sometimes, you don't have to say a word.

"I hate to be the bearer of bad news, but my husband might have fucked your wife," she said.

Her words were chilling and they went through my heart like a sharp knife. The thought of Trice letting another man make love to her made me sick to my stomach. Not only was this man a homeboy of mine, but we also grew up in the same neighborhood. So this was a crucial situation. I tried not to wrap my mind around the idea. Charlene was upset and pissed off, and worse, her ghetto ass wasn't making it any easier for me.

The thought of it was too painful to digest. "Look, Charlene, I know you're upset, but you can't be going around making accusations like that, especially if you don't have any facts. You know you can get people killed when you start saying shit like that."

She looked at me as if I said something wrong. "Look, I know my husband," she began. "And I know what that muthafucka is capable of doing. He has already cheated on me with a whole bunch of bitches. And believe me when I tell you that your wife is going to be next if he ain't already done her by now."

I knew I had to defend my wife's honor. Trice had never stepped out on me during our entire marriage. In spite of all the arguments we've had, I knew she wouldn't fuck around on me. I had always been the cheater in our relationship and crept around on her with a flock of chicken-head bitches from the streets. So once again, if the cheating occurred in our marriage, it would be me not her.

"Charlene, I know my wife, and I know she wouldn't sleep with Leon. Now, maybe Leon has screwed around on you with other chicks, but me and him are like blood, so I would bet money that he wouldn't cross that line with

Trice. I just know he wouldn't," I replied, trying to convince her.

It became obvious that what I said went through one ear and out the other, because she kept pressing the issue. She turned completely around and faced me. And as she poured her heart out to me, I began to feel sorry for her.

"I know Leon has probably told you that I bitch at him all the time and that I don't want to work or cook. But guess what? He made me like that," she explained, on the verge of tears. "When me and him first got together, I did everything for him. He didn't have to lift a finger to do a damn thing around our house. But after I started finding phone numbers and bitches started calling him all times of the night, I shut everything down. I wasn't about to let him continue to make a fool of me while I was playing Susie Home-maker. So, I stopped cooking, I stopped cleaning up behind him, and I stopped helping him pay the fucking bills."

"Damn, that is fucked up."

"Exactly. So why let him have his cake and eat it too?"

"I'm feeling you. But how did you two get past it?"

"Well, after I found out about the first two chicks, I forgave him and tried to put it behind us. But six months later he was back on the streets, fucking with another ho. And then after her, he picked up another one. I swear, after a while I couldn't keep up with him. It seemed like he was switching fuck partners every four to five months. And what finally broke me down was the fact that he didn't have enough respect for me to hide it. If one of them called, he would talk to them right in my face."

Tears fell down her cheeks. I didn't have any tissue around, so I got up and left her in the TV room while I retrieved a few sheets of paper towels from the kitchen. When I returned, I handed them to her. She continued to pour her heart out to me and then she apologized for trying to seduce me the night before.

"I am so sorry for the way I acted last night and this morning. I only did it because I wanted to be in the arms of a man. I am a very lonely woman."

"You don't have to apologize. Everything is cool," I told her in an effort to downplay what happened between us.

She wiped the tears from her eyes. "Well, I appreciate you saying that, but I still had to get that off my chest."

I reached over and patted her on the back. "You good. So don't continue to sweat it."

"Can I ask you a personal question?" she asked me.

"It depends on the question," I replied hesitantly.

"Have you ever cheated on your wife?"

I took a deep breath as I contemplated on whether it would be in my best interest to divulge that type of information to her. She didn't know this, but I had already known about all the chicks Leon fucked with behind her back. But the thought of her feeling as if she could confide in me about the problems in her marriage got me to feeling a little vulnerable. Then I thought about me digging a hole for myself by letting the skeletons out of my closet. She seemed like she was cool and all, but I figured if I showed her my cards, I wouldn't have any fighting power, especially if my shit hit the fan.

"I came close to doing it a few years back. But I walked away," I lied.

"What made you turn the woman down and walk away?" she probed.

"Because I wasn't trying to risk losing my wife," my lies continued.

Charlene began to sob uncontrollably. "Why can't Leon be more like you?"

I reached over with both arms and hugged her. "Not all men are the same," I replied.

While I embraced her, she placed her arms around me and held me tight. "Please don't let me go," she begged.

I could feel her heart beating as the shoulder of my shirt became saturated with her tears. She was really distraught. After holding her in my arms for more than five minutes, I began to really feel bad for her. The fact she smelled really good started getting me aroused, so I released my hold on her and gradually pulled back. She released her hold on me as well, but I could tell that wasn't what she wanted to do. I realized if I would have held her for another hour, then she would have been fine. However, it didn't slip past me that she had put me in another awkward situation. I played it off very casually.

"Do you think you're going to need some more napkins?" I asked her.

"No, I'm fine," she assured me. So I sat back on the sofa and occasionally rubbed her back. I wanted her to feel like I was there for her and that everything would be all right.

I, on the other hand, wasn't all right. I tried to block out the thought of Leon fucking Trice, but I couldn't. It wasn't cool to fuck with a nigga's emotions, so I was kind of fucked up in the head after Charlene dropped the bomb on me. I've known Leon for a while, and the nigga I know wouldn't do that to me. He wore a badge of honor around me, so I've never seen that side of him. He was cool with me. We looked out for each other. That was our bond. And I refused to believe otherwise. *But was I wrong?*

8

Trice

Leon and I caught an early matinee at Lynnhaven Mall. We saw the movie *Think Like a Man Too*. I have to admit it was a damn good movie. But what really surprised me was the fact that Leon wanted to see it more than me. After we walked out of the theater, I noticed him pressing down on the power button of his cell phone.

"You turning your phone off?" I asked him.

"Nah. I just turned it back on," he told me. "Charlene called me with a whole bunch of drama before we left the house."

Before I could make a comment, his phone began beeping. He looked down at it. "She sent me a text message," he said, and then he looked down at it closer.

"She probably wanted to tell you that she loved you," I commented.

He chuckled. "Nah, she definitely didn't tell me that. She cursed my ass out! She said she's over my shit and that I can keep showing off around you if I wanted, because when she comes back home, shit is going to change."

"When did you show off around me?" I asked him.

"I'm assuming she thought that when she and I talked earlier, you were listening to our conversation."

"Why would she think that?"

Leon stuck his phone back into the holster attached to his belt. "I don't know. And I'm not gonna give it much more thought than that."

I cracked a smile. "As you wish," I replied.

He reached over and tried to tickle me in my left side. "You being sarcastic?" He smiled.

I jumped before he could penetrate me with his fingers. "And what if I was?" I replied.

He made a break toward me, and I shot off in the opposite direction. We were literally running in the mall. We had run about thirty feet before I stopped in my tracks. It was kind of weird, but I wanted him to catch me. He grabbed me around the waist and pulled me into his arms. Now, I can't tell you how this happened, but when he grabbed a hold of me, he somehow positioned me to step backward, allowing my butt to press against his dick. It happened so quickly. So when I felt his meat had become erect at the mere touch of my ass, a tingly feeling shot through my body. I couldn't believe it, but my pussy got soaked in a matter of seconds. I felt like a fucking high school girl again, allowing my high school crush to grind on my booty.

But I snapped back to reality and realized I was in the arms of my husband's friend. A guy he grew up with, and I felt as if I were forbidden fruit. But then the strong urge inside of me surfaced and dared me to explore this new territory. *Should I give in to this emotion or not?* While I mulled over the situation, I eased my ass away from Leon's groin. I played it off with charm.

"Wanna get something to eat?" I asked him, hoping it would turn his attention away from what had just happened.

I noticed how he discreetly placed his right hand over the bulge in his pants. I acted as if I had not seen it because I was sure he was embarrassed enough.

"Yeah, sure. Where you wanna go?" he finally responded as he walked in the direction of the food court, which was in the middle of the mall.

"It really doesn't matter to me," I acknowledged as I walked alongside him. When we approached the entryway of the food court, we looked at all the selections from where we stood and decided that we were going to leave the mall and stop at an Applebee's.

A few minutes into the drive, my cell phone started ringing. I knew it was my husband, Troy, so I answered it after the first ring. "Hello."

"Whatcha doing?" he didn't hesitate to ask me.

"On my way to Applebee's with Leon," I told him.

"Y'all in the car?"

"Yeah. Why?"

"Just asking."

"Are you still at work?" I wanted to know.

"I just got off."

"I thought you were working until three."

"They let me off early."

"Well, what are you getting ready to get into?"

"I don't know. I'll probably go back to the house and throw some leftovers in the microwave. But other than that, I'm just gonna chill."

"How are you and Charlene getting along?"

"She's cool. You know me, I don't talk much. I miss the hell out of you, though."

"Oh, that's so sweet!"

"Tell Leon I said what's up."

I looked back at Leon while he was driving and told him what Troy said. "Tell 'im I said what's up."

"Leon said what's up, baby."

"You keeping it tight for me?"

"Keeping what tight?" I asked him, because I was taken aback with that question. I had no idea what the hell he was talking about.

"Nothing," he said, sounding somewhat irritated. "Tell Leon that Charlene was trying to call him earlier."

"He knows that already."

"How do you know?" Troy snapped.

"Because she sent him a text message."

"Don't get in the middle of their shit!" he warned me.

"I'm not."

"A'ight. Well, call me back after y'all finish eating."

"Okay."

By the time Troy and I finished our conversation, Leon had gotten us into the parking lot of Applebee's. Like a gentleman, he got out of the car and came around to the passenger side and opened the door for me.

"Thank you," I said.

"You're welcome," he replied.

Inside the restaurant, we were shown to our table and the waitress immediately took our drink order. While we waited for her to return, Leon thought it was necessary to ask me about my conversation with Troy.

"So what's up with Troy?"

"What do you mean?"

"I noticed how the tone of your voice changed a couple of times while y'all were talking. So I was just wondering if was he all right."

I knew deep in my heart that Troy wasn't all right. He knew I knew what was going on between Charlene and Leon, and he hated when I got involved in other people's shit. Not only that, but also I knew the idea of Leon and I going out made him feel him uneasy, which was why he asked me if I'd been keeping it tight. Keeping it tight meant was I keeping my pussy to myself.

But for the life of me I couldn't figure out why he had asked me something like that. I hadn't cheated on him the whole time we've been together. Since I was young, I had always heard that when your man or woman questions you about cheating, nine times out of ten it means they're the ones who were actually doing it. Now, if that was the case, I would truly hate it for him . . . because I would pack my bags immediately. The next time he saw me would be at divorce court. So he'd better take his own advice and keep it tight himself.

"Yeah, he's fine," I finally said.

Leon chuckled. "Well, why did he tell you to keep it tight?"

"I'm not sure," I answered him without looking him directly in the eyes. I tried avoiding eye contact with him by looking at my glass. I tend to appear as if I'm lying when I look into a person's eyes.

"Come on, you can tell me." He smiled and reached over and grabbed my hand.

I cracked a smile immediately after I looked up at him. I tried to snatch my hand away from him, but he wouldn't let my hand go.

"You know your friend. So I don't have to tell you anything," I told him.

He let my hand go very easy. "Sounds like he's missing you."

"Wouldn't you?" I replied in a flirtatious way.

"You damn right! Shit! Look at you! You're beautiful! You're intelligent. And you're down to earth. You're a woman that every man dreams of having."

"Yeah, right. Don't try to blow my head up."

"I'm dead serious," he began. "I remember when Troy first met you. He called me and talked to me for about twenty minutes bragging about how pretty and sexy you were. And then when you paid for dinner on y'all first date, he called me and told me that too."

I started blushing. "You're lying! He told you that?"

"Yeah, he did. And I can't lie, I was jealous."

"Why?"

"Because I had been dating some airhead chicks."

I blushed even harder. It felt really good to hear how jealous he was when he found out about Troy's and my relationship. I was even flattered to know how ecstatic Troy had been that he'd met me. Men normally don't run and tell their friends about every woman they meet. Women do it all the time. But I guess I was an exception being as I had excellent qualities without the baggage.

"Well, you don't have an airhead chick now," I commented, knowing exactly how he really felt about his wife. But the plan was for me to get the attention off me.

"Whatcha got, jokes? I married the biggest airhead in the world."

"Oh, stop it, Leon. I'm sure she's a sweetheart."

"She used to be. But that was many moons ago."

"I'm sure it was," I replied sarcastically. I found that men are always trying to make their wives sound like naggers. They always play the victim role too. But if they would only do what they are supposed to do, then they would have a good wife. What they say is true: *A happy wife makes a happy house.*

"You just don't understand what I go through,"

he continued in an effort to convince me about the turmoil in his marriage. But I was no dummy. There were always two sides to every story. And right now I was hearing Leon's side, so I knew he was pouring the drama on really thick.

After I listened to him beat me in the head with all the mess he said Charlene took him through, I ate my food. What was left of it I got the waitress to put in a to-go box. On the way back to Leon's house, I got him to drive by my house. It was a last-minute request, but he happily obliged. He did mention we wouldn't be able to stop because of the "no physical contact rule" that was imposed.

During the entire seven days, we were prohibited to have any physical contact with our significant others or we would forfeit the $10,000 at the end of the week. I wasn't too happy about the rule when the people ran down everything to us. But Troy had me focus on the reward at the end of this journey, so that's what I was doing.

It was around four-thirty in the afternoon and the sun was up for everyone to see it. I sat back in the passenger seat of Leon's vehicle as we drove through my neighborhood. I saw a few people I knew from my community, but I didn't allow them to see me. It would've been somewhat odd for them to see me in a car with another man. And since I wasn't in the mood to explain myself to them, I kept out of sight. I hoped Troy did the same with Charlene. I really didn't feel like explaining myself to my neighbor, Ashley. She was a noisy bitch, and she knew how to put a person's business out among the other neighbors. I was surprised she hadn't gotten her ass kicked yet. But don't rule me out, because in the back of my head, I thought I might be the first to do it.

When Leon arrived within a few yards of my street, I asked him to slow down so I could get a good look at the house. I only needed to see it because I missed it. So as he slowed down, I took a mental picture of the house and the landscape around it. Everything was exactly how I had left it. The only thing that stood out for me was the fact that I wasn't there.

I noticed Troy wasn't there either. So I pulled out my phone and called him immediately. The phone rang at least five times before it went to voice mail. I didn't feel like leaving him a voice mail, so I disconnected the call. I didn't say anything to Leon about it, but I wondered why he didn't answer my call. I also wondered where he and Charlene could be. I guess I would find out later.

After Leon left my block, he put the pedal to the metal and drove us back to his place in Norfolk. We didn't talk much from my house to his. It seemed like both of our spouses had us in deep thought.

Trading Spouses *might have been a bad move after all.*

9

Leon

As soon as Trice and I arrived back at my house, my cell phone started ringing. I started not to answer it when I saw Charlene's name pop up on the caller ID. But I knew she would continue to blow my phone up until I answered it.

"Yeah, what's up?" I answered nonchalantly. I let her know right off the bat that I was not feeling the idea of her calling me right now. She caught on to my tone of voice immediately.

"What the fuck you mean what's up? I'm not your homeboy!" she roared.

"I didn't say that you were," I replied. But I was completely annoyed at the sound of her voice.

"Well, why the hell are you talking to me like that? You know I don't play that shit. Talk to me like I'm your wife."

"What do you want?" I snapped at her. She was plucking my fucking nerves, and I wanted her to get to the point as to why she called me in the first place.

"Leon, don't play stupid! You know why I called you. I mean, you did hang up on me earlier. So, do you think I'm over that?"

"You should be. That shit happened this morning."

"Keep showing off!"

"How the fuck am I showing off, Charlene? You're talking really reckless right now."

"Nigga, you're the one talking reckless. But it's all good because when all of this shit is over, I will get some payback."

"Yeah, yeah, yeah. Are you through?" I replied sarcastically. At that point, I was ready to hang up on her. I had just gotten home from an early lunch with Trice, and I wasn't in the mood to argue with Charlene. She knew what to say to press my buttons, and I couldn't let her bring me out of my shell right now. I didn't want Trice to see me in rare form. So I politely disconnected the call while she was screaming through the phone. Thankfully, Trice was in the bathroom while all of this was going on. I knew if I would've stayed on the phone and entertained

Charlene just a little bit longer, then Trice would have heard all the chaos.

When she exited the bathroom, she rubbed her stomach in a circular motion. "Boy, am I full. That shrimp and spinach salad was delicious. And the glazed chicken breast was even better."

"My food was good too. Too bad I don't have any leftovers," I commented as I led the way to the TV room.

"You can have some of mine," she offered.

"That's good to know," I told her, and then we settled down on the sofa.

And right before Trice was about to say something back to me, my cell phone started ringing again. I let out a loud sigh because I knew it was none other than my worrisome-ass wife. She had become more of a pain in my ass gone than she was when she was here. I honestly wanted to ignore the call, but again, I knew if I had done that, then she would continue to call me if I didn't answer.

As I pulled my phone from my pocket, I noticed it wasn't Charlene calling me. It was this chick I used to fuck named Sabrina. She was a bad chick, pretty as hell with a tiny waist and a fat ass. She had the proper ingredients for a one-night stand. The only downside to her was that she was too needy. Plus, the bitch didn't have any money, and she lived with her mama in

Young's Park. She was the type of chick that would let a nigga sell her a dream about how much he loved her, that he would take her out of the projects and give her all the nice things she desired. She was very naïve.

I was able to tell her exactly that and fuck her the same night I met her. And I had to admit that her pussy was good. I swear I had not met another woman yet whose pussy could stay wet longer than hers. Not to mention she could suck the skin off a nigga's dick. I almost pulled her fucking weave out of her head that first night.

But as soon as I got my nut off, I was ready to send her on her way. Her conversation game was zero, and she had absolutely no ambition. All she talked about was how she needed a car and couldn't wait until her section eight crib came through. Believe me when I tell you that I was completely turned off, and I skated from her ass right after I washed my dick off. Too bad she didn't have a bit of common sense. Hell, if she did, she would be a bad bitch.

"Hello," I said as I got up from the sofa. I didn't want Trice to hear another woman's voice.

"Whatcha doing, stranger?" she asked.

I waited until I reached the hallway before I responded. "I'm cool. And you?" I replied.

"I'm okay. But I'm missing you."

I walked out the front door and closed it behind me. "I miss you too," I told her, even though it was a lie. I knew I could tell this chick the sky was falling and she'd believe me. She was just that gullible.

"So, when can I see you?" she got straight to the point.

"I can't say right now because I'm out of town," my lies continued.

"Damn, Leon, you are always out of town," she whined. "When will you come back this time?"

"I told you how my job keeps me traveling."

She sighed. "I know. But I was hoping that I'd catch you and you'd be able to come and see me."

"I'll be back in a couple of weeks."

"You promise you're gonna call me when you get back?"

"Yeah, I promise."

"Well, you better because this pussy needs you. It's been real lonely since you've been gone."

I laughed. "I'll make it up to you."

"I'ma hold you to that."

"A'ight. I'll holla at you later."

"Okay."

After I disconnected the call from Sabrina, I hauled ass back into the house. On the way down the hall, I heard Trice talking. As I got closer to the TV room, it became obvious who she was talking to. She sounded irritated, so I made a detour to the kitchen to give her some privacy. While I was in the kitchen, I could hear bits and pieces of her conversation. She tried to talk as quietly as she could, but like a nosy neighbor, I had my ears glued to the wall. I knew what was going on.

I knew Troy was starting to have some reservations about this arrangement, because he hasn't stopped calling since this whole thing started. He knew from day one that I was a womanizer. He and I have had our share of women. We talked about it all the time while we were working. He knew I could fuck any chick I wanted. So I'm assuming the fact that I had his woman in my company was making him feel uneasy. And as guarded as Troy was, he wouldn't bring that issue to my attention. Troy had a lot of pride . . . and he wouldn't let anyone know his weaknesses or when he was hurt. He knew I wasn't the type of man who would force anyone to talk to me about their problems, so if he didn't pick up the phone to call me, then I wouldn't call him.

After Trice got off the phone, she walked into the kitchen where I was. She stood before me as if she had fifty-pound weights on her shoulders.

"What's wrong?" I asked.

"Troy is acting crazy. He's worried to death about what I am doing. And I keep telling him that I'm not doing anything. But for some reason, it's not registering in that thick skull of his."

"Can you blame the man? I mean, look at you!" I replied, and cracked a big smile.

"Stop it. I'm trying to be serious, Leon," she whined.

I grabbed her by both her shoulders. "I know you're being serious. But I've known your husband longer than you. You should know that you ain't gon' win every battle with him. Just give him some space and let him ponder for a while. Then he'll figure it out and snap out of it."

"You think so?"

"I know so. Now let's go watch some TV."

I watched Trice from my peripheral vision as she watched the show on TV. She tried to concentrate, but she couldn't. Troy was stressing her out. And who could blame him? Because deep down inside my heart, I wanted his wife. She didn't know it, but he and I knew it. *And as much as I wanted to, I couldn't deny my feelings.*

10

Charlene

I think I cried so much that I developed a fuck-ing headache. I asked Troy for a couple of Tylenol and a glass of water. Within seconds, he was handing me a cold bottle of spring water and two aspirins. I popped the pills in my mouth without even thinking about it. Then I laid my head back against the headrest of the sofa in the den. I closed my eyes and wondered how I could make my life just a little more stress-free. I was finally tired of all the hustle and bustle of life. I was even more tired of my cheating-ass husband. I knew years ago that this day would come. I'd tried to delay the inevitable by putting up with all his shit. But that was over now. It was time to cut my losses and time for a new beginning.

When this whole wife swap thing was over, I was gonna get some payback and then I was getting as far away from Leon as I possibly could.

While I was in deep thought planning my escape, Troy tapped me on the leg to see if I was awake. I opened my eyes and lifted my head. "Yeah, I'm awake. What's up?"

"How is your head feeling?" he asked me as he stood up before me.

"The aspirins are starting to work. That's why I laid my head back against the sofa."

"Well, I'm about to go out to my garage and straighten up a few things, but if you need me, just holla."

"Okay. I sure will," I assured him. I watched him as he walked away.

Fifteen minutes after Troy left for the garage, I heard his cell ringing. Evidently he had left it in the kitchen. It rang five times and stopped. I assumed that whoever made the call left him a voice mail. But a minute later, the phone began ringing again. I got up this time. I felt as if whoever was calling him must've really wanted to talk to him. When I got to the kitchen, I picked up the phone and noticed the call was coming from his wife, Trice. I stared at the caller ID, trying to decide whether to answer it. I finally picked it up before it stopped ringing and said hello.

She hesitated for a brief moment, before saying, "Who is this?"

I had every right to give her a dumb-ass answer for that dumb-ass question. I mean, who in the hell could it be other than me? I was the only woman in her husband's company. Was she trying to be funny or what? She couldn't be that fucking stupid. Or did she make the mistake by asking me the wrong question? Because, if it were me, I would've been straight up with her and asked her why was she answering my husband's phone. But I guess she wasn't built like me. I was a hood chick and hood chicks didn't play when it came to our men.

"It's Charlene," I finally said.

"Where is my husband?" she asked in an irritated manner.

"He's indisposed right now," I lied. I wanted to see how long she would let me play this game with her. The way I looked at it, being indisposed could mean a lot of things. But since I was at her house with her husband, indisposed meant he couldn't come to the phone because he was busy doing something he wasn't supposed to be doing.

"Indisposed!" she screeched. "You tell him to get on the phone now!" she demanded.

I could tell she was getting really pissed off. I started to laugh in her ear and tell her I was only joking, but I was getting a kick out of fucking with her emotions. Besides, I wanted her to get a taste of how I felt when my husband fucked around with my emotions. I was tired of being the only chick with an asshole for a husband.

"I wish I could, but he told me if somebody called him to take a message," I replied nonchalantly.

"Girl, I'm not trying to hear that bullshit. Put my husband on the phone right now!" she demanded.

Again, I wanted to laugh in her ear because she was feeding into my drama and I was loving it. But I didn't want to give her the impression that I was being immature, so I held back and continued to pour more fuel on the fire.

"Sweetheart, don't shoot me! I'm just the messenger," I replied calmly.

"Well, I was told by your husband that you're more like a hood rat bitch with low self-esteem and no education!" she snapped.

No this bitch didn't just tell me that Leon called me a hood rat bitch with low self-esteem and no education. I was shocked and completely caught off guard by her comment. I hadn't clocked another bitch in a long time, but I wanted to beat this bitch's ass for disrespecting me. Maybe I shouldn't have been fucking with her the way I was, but now I didn't have a choice—I had to continue the game, especially after she made it personal. I had to come back at her ass real hard now. I couldn't dare let her get away with insults like that.

"Well, my husband might think I'm a hood rat bitch, but your husband thinks I'm a down-to-earth ride-or-die chick. As a matter of fact, he thinks the world of me. And just a minute ago he kissed me on the mouth and told me that I threw my pussy on him better than you could. So you see, Ms. Goody Two-shoes, I may be a bitch to you and my husband, but I'm the best thing that your husband has ever had."

"Oh really? So you're saying you and my husband fucked, huh?"

"Oops! I'm sorry! Did I just say that?" I chuckled.

"So this is a game to you, huh?" she said, but I could hear the aggravation in her tone. She was livid with me. And I'm assuming she was heartbroken at the thought of Troy fucking me. Shit, I was heartbroken when I found out about all the bitches Leon fucked. The sisterly thing to do was to understand her feelings. Hell, I didn't or couldn't feel sorry for her in the least bit. People say misery loves company. And they were right. My misery was lonely as hell and company had just walked in the door.

"No, Trice, this is not a game. We are all adults, sweetie. So put an *H* on your chest, baby girl, and handle it. Shit, men fuck around on their wives all the time. It didn't start with you and it ain't gonna end with you. The faster you get over this, the better off you'll be."

"Bitch, you must think I am crazy! See, the difference between you and I is that I come from a good family with strong morals and values. And you come from the slums. So I don't have to deal with a goddamn thing! I know who I am. So, bitch, I know my worth. Now, if my husband wants to jeopardize our union because of some chicken-head bitch with dick breath and sloppy pussy, then that's fine with me. And as far as your husband is concerned, I'm starting to feel really sorry for him because he's a really good man. Not to mention, now I can see why he salivates when I come within two feet of him. He's not used to being around a real woman with class."

"Bitch, please! You ain't got no class! You just like all the other chicks around here."

"Don't let the good girl image fool you, Charlene. If you and I walked down the street together, I would get all of the attention. So face it, you can't hold a candle to me. I'm not in your class. And speaking of which, I just now had to remind myself that I am wasting my time with you. You are beneath me."

"Wow! What a coincidence. I'm beneath you and just a minute ago I was beneath your husband while he was on top of me sliding his dick in and out of my wet, juicy pussy."

"Well, I hope you made him use a condom because if you didn't, join the club. Because now you got the herpes just like us," she replied, and hung up.

Immediately after she hung up, Troy walked back into the house. He startled the hell out of me, but I had enough time to stuff his Black-Berry down into my pocket. I couldn't let him see it in my hands.

I was standing in front of the kitchen island when he approached me. "You seen my phone?" he asked.

My heart started racing. I didn't know whether to tell him I had his phone or act as if I hadn't seen it. But while I thought about what to say, I hoped and prayed that his phone didn't ring while I had it buried inside my pocket. I quickly told him I hadn't seen his phone and then asked him to excuse me while I went to the bathroom. Thank God he bought my story and moved out of my way so I could pass him.

I rushed down the hallway and into the hall bathroom. After I closed the door behind me, I took his phone from my pocket and turned the power off. I couldn't let him get a chance to talk to his wife, especially after the conversation she and I had just had. If he found out what I told her this early in the game, he would surely throw my ass out of his house. So I thought of a plan to make him think he either lost his phone or misplaced it until I was able to lure him into my trap. I had already told his wife he and I had had sex, so I had to find a way to make it happen before she found out otherwise. So immediately after I turned the power off on his phone, I stuck it back into my pocket and left the bathroom.

Troy had made his way back to the garage. I could hear him rambling through some things out there. I figured he thought he left his phone in the garage. That's how I wanted to keep it.

While I was trying to regroup, I heard my phone beep. The chirping sound told me someone had texted me. I looked at my cell phone to see who had texted me and when I realized it came from Leon, my heart jumped and I got an uneasy feeling in the pit of my stomach.

I heard u got ur rocks off, bitch! I hope it was worth it. 'Cause u can't come home, the text message read.

My mouth shot wide open. I shouldn't have been surprised. I knew Trice was going to go back and repeat what I said to her, so that didn't faze me one bit. But what I did care about was the fact that he'd text me and tell me I couldn't come home. Was he off his motherfucking rocker? I've endured countless episodes of his cheating and the first time he heard that I might have cheated on him, he threatens to kick me out of our house. Was he insane? But I knew he was a fucking coward. The least he could've done was call me instead of texting me. I wasn't standing for his bullshit anymore. And I wasn't going to let this shit stress me out. Trice was gonna have to prove I said all that stuff to her. I wasn't admitting to anything until I got my half of the $10,000. Once that happened, I would tell him to kiss my ass all the way to the bank.

11

Trice

I was a big ball of tears when I got off the phone with Charlene. She was a fucking monster with no heart. If I were in front of her trifling ass, I would've scratched her fucking eyes out of her head. I mean, how dare she talk shit to me and tell me she had just fucked my husband? Talk about being bold. That ho was definitely a bold bitch. But what really added insult to injury was that Troy told her to tell anyone that called that he was indisposed and for her to take a message. I was his wife, not his fucking girlfriend or his mistress. So how disrespectful was that?

I was sitting on the edge of the bed contemplating on whether I should call Troy and confront him when Leon appeared at the doorway of his son's bedroom. "I texted Charlene and told her she couldn't bring her ass home," Leon spat.

He took my mind off Troy for the moment. "I thought you were going to call her," I replied.

He stood at the door with his arms folded and said, "I started to but I didn't want to hear her fucking lies, so I decided not to."

"What would make her be so bold and say all those things to me? I mean, what kind of person is she?"

"I already told you how she is. She's a heartless bitch! And she doesn't care about anyone but herself."

"Well, let's not forget the bastard I am married to. Remember, it takes two, and she didn't get laid by herself," I acknowledged. I said that because Troy had as much to do with what they did as she did. They were both to blame, so why should Leon and I throw all the stones at Charlene?

Leon shook his head with disgust. He seemed like he was more hurt than I was in spite of all the claims he made about how he wanted to leave her. I had been told that when a man found out his woman had given her goodies to another man or to make it worse, a cat they grew up with in grade school, then that man felt less than a man. Regardless if that man was the biggest ho in the world, his pride and dignity took a major hit. He was no longer the big dawg. Now he was the little pup with a cup to pee in, and not the huge toilet bowl that men pissed in.

Men had pride issues while women were more emotional and vocal. Men were logical and tried not to deal with their emotions. Because of this perceived toughness and stowing those feelings internally, their emotions hit them harder. The lion's heart was replaced with that of a pussycat.

"Yeah, I know, but she probably came on to him," he said, defending Troy. But I wasn't trying to hear that bullshit. Both of them were to blame.

"It doesn't matter who did what," I stated. "They both are at fault."

"Are you going to try and call him again?"

"For what? So he can lie?" I replied. "I'm not in the mood for lies right now, Leon. I swear my heart isn't going to be able to take it. All I wanna do right now is lie down and figure out how I am going to handle this situation when I get home."

I was on the verge of tears. My eyes were filling up very quickly. So I reached up and wiped them with the back of my hand.

"What if he calls you?"

"I'm not gonna talk to him," I said as the tears streamed down my face.

Leon walked over to me and took a seat next to me on the bed. Then he placed his arm around me. In turn, I buried my face in his chest and let all my emotions flow. I sobbed like I had lost Troy to death. And in all honesty, it really felt like a part of me had died.

The feeling of betrayal and infidelity ripped my heart apart at the seams while Leon held me in his arms. I believe the only thing that saved me from having a nervous breakdown at that moment was Leon whispering in my ear that it was okay to cry and that I would be all right. This was death, the death of my marriage, and Leon was the comforter.

I believe Leon and I stayed embraced for more than twenty minutes. Him holding me the way he did made me feel as if he was there to protect me, and honestly, I didn't want him to let me go.

"You are going to be all right, baby. Watch and see," Leon assured me.

When I finally got myself together and felt that I did enough crying, I asked Leon to let me get some rest. He happily obliged and left the room. Immediately after he closed the bedroom door, I turned off my cell phone. I didn't want to hear from Troy at all. I had heard enough shit from Charlene. Now what I needed to do was have some alone time so I could figure out how to approach this situation when it was time to go home.

12

Troy

I couldn't figure out for the life of me where my cell phone was. I couldn't remember where I had put it. I thought if I called it using the house phone it would ring and I could locate it. Surprisingly, it didn't ring. As a matter of fact, my phone went straight to voice mail, which led me to believe that the battery had to be dead. Now I knew Trice must have called me by now. And if she got my voice mail, I knew she wasn't going to be a happy camper about it. If you want to know the truth, I wouldn't be happy if I called her and her phone kept going straight to voice mail. And being at my homeboy's house wouldn't make the situation any better.

Knowing how Leon was with a vulnerable

woman wasn't a pretty sight . . . especially if the woman was someone you loved—like I loved Trice. So to keep my mind at ease, I picked up the house phone and tried to get her on the line so I could explain to her that I misplaced my phone and couldn't find it.

Unfortunately for me, her phone went straight to voice mail as well. Now I figured that either she was trying to dial out the same time I was or she turned her phone off. I pressed the redial button and when the line connected, her voice mail came on instantly.

"Wait a minute, what the fuck is going on?" I said aloud, but low enough so Charlene couldn't hear me.

I waited several seconds after I cleared the phone line and dialed her number manually instead of pressing the redial button. But that didn't help because I still couldn't get a connection. Her line went straight to voice mail yet again and I got pretty upset about it. I wanted to slam the phone down, but I knew it wouldn't do any good. I remained calm and thought of another way to get in touch with my wife. I placed the phone back in the base and strolled into the den where Charlene was. She was sitting on the recliner watching TV.

"Can you please do me a favor?" I asked her.

"Yeah, what's up?"

"Could you call Leon and ask him to put Trice on the phone for me?"

Charlene looked at me in a weird way. She acted as if I had said something wrong. I guess she figured out I really wanted to talk to my wife, so she pulled out her phone and made the call. She put her cell against her ear and waited. Several seconds later she pulled the phone away from her ear and pressed the END button.

"What happened?"

"He must've turned his phone off because it went straight to voice mail."

My heart sank to the pit of my stomach after hearing Charlene's response. All I could think about was why both of their phones were off. *What in the world could they be doing? I mean, what was going on? Could it be a mere coincidence? Or were they doing something they shouldn't be doing?*

Charlene had her own take on the situation. She gave me this uncertain look and said, "You ain't gotta say a word, but I know what you're thinking."

I didn't respond. My heart wouldn't let me. My pride consumed my entire body. But that didn't stop Charlene from running her mouth.

"Don't you think it's strange that we can't get in touch with them?" she continued.

I continued to stand there speechless.

"I know it's hard for you to believe it, but I

know what my husband is capable of doing. So I know what's up. It wouldn't shock me if he had her in our bed breaking her back out right now."

"Nah, I know Trice. She wouldn't do that," I finally spoke up in my wife's defense. I couldn't let Charlene convince me otherwise. I knew how I was when it came to protecting people I loved. I'd go off on a killing spree if I believed wholeheartedly Leon was fucking my wife. I couldn't just let him disrespect me like that and not do anything about it. No way.

Charlene stood to her feet. "Well, that may be true, but don't forget who she's with. Leon is a womanizer. And he doesn't discriminate when it comes to pussy. So while you're standing there rooting for your wife, she's over at my house doing her thing with my husband and they aren't thinking about either of us."

I tried to come back at Charlene. But I couldn't think of the words to say. She shot down every possibility I had bottled up in my head. And what was so frustrating about it was that she had hit the nail on the head. Leon was a dog. He loved the chase of hunting new women, especially if they looked good and were sexy. It didn't matter if they had a man. He welcomed the challenge of taking another man's property. Homeboy or not, I wasn't an exception.

Instead of feeding into Charlene's antics, I

grabbed the cordless phone from the end table next to the love seat and began to dial Trice's number again. I wasn't ready to believe Leon was fucking the brains out of my wife. *No way.*

"Who are you calling?" Charlene asked me. She looked a bit worried. But I had to admit I was more worried than she was.

"I'm calling Trice again."

Charlene took two steps toward me and leaned her ear near my phone. She didn't have to lean close for long, because as soon as the line connected, it once again went directly to voice mail. I started to leave her a message, but I decided against it. I knew she was bad about checking her messages. So I pressed the OFF button and placed the phone back in its base.

Charlene looked at me and shook her head. "The voice mail picked up again, huh?"

"Yeah," I replied, and then I dropped my head.

I sat back down on the sofa and laid my head against the headrest. I was so devastated at the thought of what could be going on at Leon's house, I wanted to hop in my truck and ride over there to see for myself. Then something inside of me told me I was being a little paranoid. I knew my wife. I knew she wouldn't dare cross the line and play herself . . . especially with my homeboy. There had to be a perfect explanation for why their phones were off. And sooner or later, I would find out what it was. I took a couple of deep breaths and tried to regroup.

Meanwhile, my eyes were closed. But not for long. I felt Charlene's hand rub my thigh. I lifted my head and opened my eyes. She had the most sympathetic look on her face.

"What are you thinking about?" she asked me.

"I'm thinking about whether or not I should take a ride over to your house."

Charlene didn't like the idea of me wanting to check up on Leon and Trice. Her whole expression changed. "That's not a good idea. You would be blowing this whole arrangement out of the water and then none of us will get our money at the end," she explained.

"Do you think I really care about that money . . . especially if there's a chance that I could lose my wife in the process?"

"Look, Troy, I understand what you are saying. But what if we did go to my house and found out that nothing is going on? We would be looking really stupid and we would also lose our money."

"Wait a minute, why you singing another tune? You were just standing in front of me saying that they were probably fucking in your bed!" I snapped. "And now you're saying that they might not be doing anything? Make up your damn mind!"

I was frustrated and I expressed it. And honestly, I was kind of tired of Charlene. I disliked being around flaky chicks and she was taking the damn cake. This was about money for her. I could use the change—hell, I was the one who thought of the idea, did the research, and contacted the show—but no way was I losing my wife in the process.

"All I'm saying is that I know my husband. I know what he's capable of doing, which is why I am going to leave his ass when all this is over. And if you say you know your wife and she wouldn't fall into Leon's trap, then I believe you. But please don't blow this thing up before its time. Leave well enough alone until we get through these last couple of days. And when it's all over, then you step up and state your claim. But for right now, let's keep our eyes on the prize. You know you and I both need that money. There's absolutely no dick on this earth worth ten grand. I don't know about you, but I've got my head on straight. Now you do the same."

"All that shit you're saying sounds good. But if there was something going on between them, I'd rather prevent it from happening in the first place. You don't have anything to lose. I do."

"Did you hear anything I just said? I just mentioned that we could forfeit ten thousand dollars if we don't play our cards right."

"Charlene, I couldn't really care less about

that fucking money," I snapped once again. This bitch had already plucked my damn nerves; now she was fucking with my patience. I was about to push her ass onto the floor. All this shit she was talking really didn't make any sense to me. One minute she was talking crazy, saying she didn't trust Leon and that I shouldn't trust him either because of all the hoes he's fucked behind her back. And then she turns around and feeds me a whole bunch of crap about how we should turn a blind eye to the possibility of her husband and my wife lying in her bed and fucking each other's brains out. But I couldn't do that. My heart wouldn't let me wait that long. I mean, I was a man with feelings. So what would be the best remedy? Let her stay there and take the risk of her sleeping with him? Or should I call this whole thing off, rescue her from that no-good-ass nigga, and cut my losses?

I knew one thing for sure: Charlene wasn't going to let me out of her sight until she could find a way to reason with me.

"Let me ask you something," she said.

"I'm listening," I replied.

"If you went by my house right now and found them having sex, what would you do?"

I thought for a second and then I said, "I can't answer that right now because I don't know."

"Do you think you would hurt Leon?" she continued.

I thought about seeing Leon on top of Trice, having his way with her. The thought got me sick to my stomach instantly. "Yeah, I probably would try to kill him with my bare hands," I finally said.

"And if you do that, you know you'll go to jail, right?"

"At that point I wouldn't care."

"But you should. Because you would lose everything you've ever worked for. And I don't think killing Leon is worth that. He's my husband and the father of my child, and I wouldn't throw my life away behind his filthy ass. So do yourself and me both a favor and let whatever is done in the dark come to light. Because I can guarantee you that if they are doing anything that they ain't supposed to be doing, it will come out. And you can take that one to the bank."

After Charlene made her point, I sat back on the sofa and thought about everything she said. And the more I thought about it, the more I realized she was right. If I went over there, I would definitely end up in jail and I didn't want that. All I needed to do was let this whole thing play out, and if something was going on over there between them, it would come out.

Once I came to terms about my decision to leave well enough alone, I closed my eyes and said a silent prayer to God. I needed God more than ever now. It would be extremely hard if I tried to do this thing alone. And things would end up deadly too. I could picture myself sticking the barrel of the gun into that nigga's mouth. I'd even pistol-whip him if he lied or disrespected me to my face. I knew I'd take pleasure in seeing this nigga beg for his life, especially if I managed to catch them two in the act. Shit would definitely turn fatal. So I say, *God, please take the wheel.*

13

Leon

Whether Charlene knew it or not, I was through with her slutty ass. I'd waited on this day for a long time and now it was finally here. I would be free at last of that lazy tramp for good. She couldn't imagine how she made my day by telling Trice that bullshit about her and Troy.

If you want to know the truth, I wasn't mad with Troy at all. He did me a favor by fucking that grimy bitch. So I was gonna get Trice to remind me to thank him later. Now, I knew she was gonna try to take me to court for child support, but I couldn't care less at this point. I would pay the dirty bitch five hundred dollars a month to stay away from her miserable ass.

Other than that, she couldn't and wouldn't get a fucking penny from me. And if she thought she was going to get a dime of the ten thousand dollars, she had another think coming. When I got through with that ho, she was gonna wish she had never met me. I was going to make her life a living hell by the time I got through with her. I didn't want to talk to her filthy ass, so I decided to keep my damn cell phone off when I wasn't using it.

Trice stayed in my son's room for at least an hour before she came back downstairs. I could tell she had cried the entire time she was up there. I wanted to comfort her when she walked into the TV room, but I allowed her to have her space. I figured if she wanted me to do something for her, she would tell me.

"I tried to get some sleep, but I couldn't stop thinking about my conversation with your wife," she said after she entered the room.

"That rat ain't my wife no more."

Trice took a seat on the sofa beside me. "I'm sorry for being so forward, but could you hold me?"

I was shocked by her question . . . and somewhat hesitant. But when I looked into her eyes and saw how hurt she was, I couldn't deny her. I reached over and placed my arm around her neck. She immediately leaned into my armpit and laid her head against my chest. The smell of her perfume did wonders for me. It was intoxicating. Not to mention it felt good to have her face pressed against my body.

"I'm filing for divorce when all of this is over," she said.

I looked down at her and saw a single tear fall down her face from each eye. She was hurt and there was no denying that.

"Don't you think you need to hear his side of the story first?" I asked her. Although Troy had stepped out on me and fucked my wife, I wasn't a hater. I really wanted Trice to think about what she was saying. I had known women to make really bad decisions when they were emotional and upset. Knowing this, I felt Trice needed to think about what she was doing long and hard before she acted, or better yet, reacted.

She lifted her head up from my chest and looked directly at me. "I know exactly what I am doing. And I should've done it a long time ago when I suspected that he fucked around on me a couple of years ago," she growled.

I threw my hands up and smiled. "Don't kill the messenger!" I said, hoping she'd smile. But it didn't work. She got more emotional. So I cradled her in my arms.

"You just don't know how hurt I am right now. I don't think I can ever speak to him."

"I know the feeling," I agreed. I was feeling the exact same way Trice was. I had no desire to ever see Charlene's face again. She had sealed her fate as far as I was concerned. I was done with her whoring ass!

Trice and I sat in that embrace for at least thirty minutes. She talked about how she was going to go on with her life after she and Troy split the money. She even talked about moving back to Florida where her parents had relocated after they retired. I listened to her map her life out while she cried her heart out. I swear I felt helpless as she lay in my arms. I wanted so badly to stop the pain she was feeling in her heart, but I knew there was nothing I could do. I did the only thing I could do—I just held her in my arms.

After a while, she stopped crying. But I had to admit that I had a hand in it. After she dried her tears, she thanked me for being there to listen to her and giving her a shoulder to cry on, and then she kissed me on the cheek. I didn't want it to stop there, so I leaned over and kissed her on the mouth. Her soft, wet lips sent sparks through my entire body. My dick got hard instantly. I believe sparks shot through her as well, because she bit down on my bottom lip very softly and then she stuck her tongue into my mouth.

I looked at her, trying to read her face, to see her expression. But she didn't have an expression. Her eyes were closed and it looked as if she were in another world. At one point I thought the kissing would stop, but it didn't. We kept alternating from kissing to sucking on one another's top and bottom lips. And it became more intense. Before I knew it, she had maneuvered her body from underneath my armpits to climbing on top of me. I found myself lying back on the sofa with her body pressed against mine. She wasn't as heavy as Charlene, so I knew I could manage her with no problem. Plus, my dick was getting more and more rock hard. I knew my little man down below would be able to handle her too.

"Please make love to me," she begged.

I mean, the words actually came out of her mouth. I couldn't believe it . . . but then again, I did. She was hurting and needed to take her mind off Troy. I guess I needed to man up for the job. She moaned between each kiss. She was hot as a fucking firecracker, and I was ready to light that fire. The warm feeling from her body rubbed off on me and made me feel as if I were on cloud nine. I had to admit that Charlene never made me feel like this. My first sexual experience with her was out of lust, but then over a period of six months I started to have feelings for her.

"Leon, I want you inside of me now," she continued to beg. Without hesitation, I turned her over on her back, pulled up her skirt, and ripped her white satin panties off. Her legs were spread-eagle, and I had a full view of her fat pussy. Instead of pulling my dick out and ramming it inside of her, I had to stick my tongue inside of her so I could taste it first.

"I gotta taste you first," I told her. Then I dove headfirst between her legs. I stretched my tongue out as long as I could and licked her entire clit. I moved my tongue around in a circular motion and she began to go crazy. She jerked her pussy back and forth like a wild child. I loved every minute of it. She made me feel as if I was the man. I was in control and that's why I was so in tune with her.

"Grind that pussy in my face," I demanded. And like a sex slave she did just that.

"Ooowwww, you make me feel so good," she moaned, and then she wrapped her legs around my head.

Moments later, I inserted two of my fingers inside of her wet pussy. She jerked instantly, giving me the green light to continue penetrating her. I pushed my fingers in and out at least ten times before she started begging me to stick my dick inside of her. I couldn't lie; I wanted her more than she appeared to want me. But I hesitated. I knew I didn't have any condoms on hand. I tried to rationalize how I would be able to fuck her without one. I wasn't trying to get her pregnant or catch something I wouldn't be able to get rid of, so I tried to hold off as long as I could by giving her as much foreplay as I possibly could. But she grew tired and begged me once more to penetrate her.

"I don't have a condom," I told her.

"I don't care. Just pull out when you're about to come," she instructed me.

Hearing her tell me to pull my dick out when I was about to bust my nut was what I already had in mind. It was a no-brainer. Going in her raw and catching AIDS or herpes was on my mind more than anything. Even though I had no intentions on going back to Charlene, I didn't want to walk away from Trice with a medical condition. That wasn't part of the plan. I had to ask her the million-dollar question.

"Is it safe?" I asked her.

She lay there and looked up at me. "Is what safe?" she asked.

"Have you been tested lately?" I replied.

She smiled. "Of course I have. Six months ago. Have you?"

Relieved by her answer, I smiled back at her. "Yeah, I was tested about ten months ago."

"Well, what are you waiting on? Show me what you got!" she continued, and then she pulled me down on her.

It only took me three seconds flat to pull my dick out and slide it deep inside her pussy. The shit was like an explosion. Her pussy was so wet and sweet that I was about to lose my fucking mind. What was so weird was that while I was fucking the hell out of her, all I could think about was how Troy would feel to know I was banging the hell out of his wife. I knew he treasured her because he always talked about how much he loved her. He even talked about how he would feel if he ever lost her. She was his prize possession. But then I had to remind myself of how foul he was for fucking my wife. So Trice was fair game.

I dug in Trice's pussy for at least thirty minutes. I had her sexy ass on her back and then I flipped her on her knees. She enjoyed it as much as I did. And right before I was about to drain my wad in Trice's fat pussy, I pulled out and beat my dick against the back of her ass until all my juices filtered out on her ass cheeks.

"Damn! I haven't been fucked like that in a very long time," she said as she reached on the floor for her panties.

I got up from the sofa and stood to my feet with my dick in my hand and gave her the biggest smile my face could muster. But what made me smile even more was when she grabbed me by my belt buckle and pulled me back in her direction. I had no idea what she was about to do until she leaned into me and grabbed my dick in her hand. Before I could say one word, she pushed the head of my dick into her mouth and then she pulled it back out real slow. I was shocked and didn't know what the fuck to say. I was glad she said something first.

"I couldn't let your precious juices drip onto the floor," she told me with a smile.

After hearing her explanation, I smiled even more. She was a bad bitch. Just like that, I was falling for her. My heart was feeling that love spark, and that type of feeling didn't come on me that easy. For some reason, I was feeling this chick. She was everything a man could ever want. I didn't want to get my hopes up, but if she dumped Troy like she said she would, I could definitely see us getting together and making some shit happen.

After all the touchy-feely shit was over, I convinced her to take a shower with me. We got in the shower and played around with each other. I mean, we were acting like teenagers who were sneaking around in their parents' house. I was cool as hell and I enjoyed every bit of it. And right after we got out of the shower, we put on some clothes to lounge around the house and then she got in the kitchen and showed me her cooking skills. She whipped up a pan of shepherd's pie with ground beef. I wasn't a fan of shepherd's pie, but this dish was good. There was nothing like getting a piece of good pussy and a hot plate of food afterward.

Trice sat across from me at the kitchen table so we could eat our food together. Charlene and I rarely if ever sat and ate together. The act of talking while you're eating an intimate dinner was good stuff. I can truthfully say that I enjoyed it.

In addition to making good food, Trice was very attentive and I loved that about her. She could even hold an intelligent conversation. She just had this presence about herself. She had the whole package.

During our dinner encounter, she and I laughed and talked about everything underneath the sun. And what was so nice about it was that I found out she and I had a lot in common. We both liked staying at home and watching movies. We liked the R&B singer Musiq Soulchild, and we both loved to cook. It seemed like she and I were perfect for each other. I even questioned why she and I hadn't met each other before we met our spouses. She didn't have an answer for me. She did what other women would do when they were put in an awkward position. There was only a matter of time before that very question would have to be answered.

As far as I was concerned, I'd trade Charlene in for Trice without hesitation. The qualities that Trice possessed over Charlene were undeniable. Boy, what I would give to change places with Troy. I knew it was a long shot, but that wouldn't stop me from dreaming.

Ain't nothing like having a bad chick on your team that the whole world could see.

14

Trice

After a hot plate of food, I settled down and thought back on how good Leon made me feel during our lovemaking session. I smiled to myself, thinking back on how I stuck Leon's dick in my mouth. I didn't know where that came from. I didn't suck Troy's dick. To do that for Leon really blew my mind. I couldn't for the life of me figure out why I did, but I didn't let it consume my thoughts.

After dinner, we got up from the table and retired to the TV room. We watched the tail end of the movie *Brooklyn's Finest*. While he was engrossed in the movie, I wondered to myself how my life would've been if I had Leon instead of Troy. I mean, he seemed like a good guy. I realized he and I had more things in common than my own husband.

Aside from the cheating and the fact that he didn't cook, Troy was a good catch as well. I just wished I had guarded my heart from him better than I did. There was no question in my mind on the day we got married that we were going to be together for the rest of our lives. I've been told that money was the root of all evil. Whoever said it was definitely right. Troy had been fixated on the idea of the trading spouse arrangement. I wasn't too keen on the idea, but normally when he said or did something, I always went along with him. And look where it got us this time.

I knew when all of this was over there would be a lot of regrets. Especially after all of the camera footage circulated. I could see Troy trying to hide his dirt. But I didn't need to see it. I heard enough from Charlene's big mouth. I didn't have any interest in rehashing anything that happened between them two. Most importantly, I knew Leon would do the same. I couldn't see him caring one way or another to see the footage from my house and I didn't blame him.

I can't speak for Charlene and Troy. They probably wanted to see what Leon and I had going on. But I didn't give a fuck. Fuck them! They could both kiss my ass. It was all about me now. I wasn't playing Ms. Goody Two-shoes any-more. Those days were long gone.

A couple of hours passed, and I found myself trying to figure out the steps I was going to make to move on with my life without Troy. I pictured him fighting me over the house, so I had already made up my mind that he could have it. All I wanted to carry away with me was half of the money we had in the account, my clothes, jewelry, and the photos of myself throughout our marriage. Anything else he could have.

Having my sanity away from Troy meant more to me than the material possessions in our house. He had hurt me for the last time. No more sleepless nights and no more heartache. How priceless was that?

The only thing I needed to figure out was where Leon and I would go from here. It wasn't hard to see that he caught feelings during our rendezvous. Shit, I caught feelings from it as well. But if I decided to run off with him, would our relationship work out? Would the grass stay green on the other side? Would he love me past all the hurt Troy had given me in my marriage? Would he be able to provide me with the lifestyle Troy had provided me with? And would he and I live happily ever after? I needed all those questions answered before I'd even considered taking that next step with Leon. I say this because my life had been one big fat hiccup. In the beginning everything started off all beautiful and wonderful. But then of course he got comfortable and started showing his ass. I'm over it. I'm tired of not getting what's owed to me. I've given Troy too many chances to get his shit straight. And now it's time to cut my ties. Who knew, maybe he and Charlene could hook up on a permanent basis. I figured they might as well since they've already tested the waters.

Fucking scavengers!

15

Charlene

Troy hadn't said anything else to me, but I heard him searching high and low for his cell phone. He tore his house upside down looking for his phone. I came really close to giving him his phone back, but I couldn't let him know I'd had it the whole time. He would have gotten rid of my ass quicker than I could blink both of my eyes.

I was still trying to get him to fuck around on his wife, but so far he had not budged. I couldn't tell you if that chick had roots on him or not, but whatever it was it had him on lock and key. His focus was on trying to find his phone so he could see if she'd tried to call him and left him a voice mail.

While he searched every crack and crevice, I sat back on the sofa and shook my head in disgust. The word *sucker* was written all over his face. Quiet as it was kept, Trice had this poor nigga wrapped around her finger. She was way across town in the house with my husband and he was walking around here like he had lost his best friend. The sight of him on this scavenger hunt was starting to get on my damn nerves. I wanted to tell him to sit his stupid ass down, but I decided against it. I was on his territory, so I knew it was best to stay in my own lane.

"This is so weird that I can't find my damn phone," he said as he looked underneath pillow cushions on the love seat and sofa.

I didn't say a word. But I did get up and act as if I was helping him look for his phone. Meanwhile, my cell phone rang. I took it from my pocket and looked at the caller ID. I didn't recognize the number, so I hesitated to answer it. But then I decided against it. I figured it might be somebody important.

"Hello," I said.

Troy stopped looking for his phone and turned his attention to me. He looked directly into my mouth. I could see it in his eyes that he hoped it was either Leon or Trice calling to talk.

"Can I speak to Lacy?" the female caller asked me.

"I'm sorry but you have the wrong number," I told her.

When I disconnected the call, Troy's questions began immediately. "Who was that?"

"I didn't get her name. But she asked to speak to somebody named Lacy. I told her she had the wrong number."

"Oh, I heard a female's voice so I thought it was Trice."

"No, it wasn't Trice," I replied nonchalantly, and then I laid my phone down on the end table next to the lamp.

Troy dropped his head and walked out of the room. I got really bored of him walking around the house as if he had just lost his best friend, so I spoke up.

"Troy, what is the deal with you? You are walking around this house like a chicken with his head cut off. You've got to lighten up. I am about to pull all of my hair out watching you walk back and forth."

"I'm sorry. It's just that I can't function without my phone. And I know Trice has probably been trying to call me. So I need to get my hands on it."

"It wouldn't surprise me if you dropped it when you were out earlier," I chimed in. I was trying to deter him from thinking that he misplaced his phone somewhere around the house. But he didn't take the bait.

"No. That can't be because the last time I remember seeing it was when I was in the kitchen getting myself a bottle of water. I swear I remember setting it down somewhere in the kitchen."

"Well, if that's what you remember, then that's where it should be," I told him.

He stood there with a clueless look on his face and said, "I've checked everywhere in there, but I couldn't find it."

I sighed. "Well, I don't know what to tell you," I told him, and then I redirected my attention to the TV. When he saw I had taken my focus off of him, he left the room and continued on with his search.

A few minutes after he left, I realized that my antics to cause problems in his marriage with Trice weren't working. This guy wouldn't stop walking around this house to look for his beat-up-ass cell phone. What kind of mind control did she have on him? Was she some kind of voodoo queen? Hell, maybe I should get into some of that shit too. I heard voodoo worked like a charm. Sprinkle a little bit of dust here and there. Take a couple strands of his hair and store it inside a bottle of solution. Or pour some magic potion into his food. I could go on and on because the list was just that long. And who knew,

I'd probably get him to pay more attention to me. And then maybe I'd be able to get him to fuck me the way I want him to.

Sounds like I've got some options.

16

Troy

I was about to take my fucking head off. I was so frustrated that I couldn't find my damn cell phone. This type of shit hadn't happened before. And it wouldn't surprise me if my phone mysteriously got up and walked off by itself. If I found out Charlene picked up and hid my phone all this time, then she was definitely going to feel my wrath. I didn't trust her. I finally understood why Leon was tired of her. I hadn't been with her the full week and I was tired of her. She was indeed a selfish bitch. It was about fucking me and getting the money. She didn't give a damn about Leon and I wasn't sure if she cared about their child.

In the meantime, I was going to use the house phone to try to get my wife back on the line. I didn't know if something was going on or if it was just bad timing. I dialed her cell phone number, and her voice mail picked up instantly. My heart dropped. I couldn't figure out why her phone kept going straight to voice mail. I knew she had her charger. Because of that, I was nervous. I hoped there was a damn good explanation for why her phone was turned off.

Instead of calling her again, I hung the phone up and got a Corona out of the refrigerator. I needed something to calm me down. I was getting pretty frustrated, and not getting the answers I was looking for wasn't sitting well with me. Immediately after I snapped the top off my beer, I took a swig and made my way back into the family room with Charlene.

"Why didn't you bring me one?" She smiled.

"Oh, my bad. I'll be right back," I assured her, and retreated back to the kitchen. I retrieved the beer from the refrigerator, opened it, and took it to her. She didn't hesitate to gulp it down after I handed it to her. I took a seat next to her and we began to drink together. One beer turned into two and two turned into three. Before we knew it, we had drunk the entire twelve-pack of Coronas. She was toasted and so was I. The alcohol completely took my mind off Trice and the fact she was over at another nigga's house.

I guess I needed something to take my mind off her. I was going crazy wondering what she was doing while I was running around here searching for a damn phone. I was okay now—or so I hoped. Those Coronas I drank got me feeling real nice. They had Charlene feeling really nice, too, because she acted as if she couldn't keep her damn hands off me. She started feeling my dick and she wouldn't stop. I had to admit that I wasn't interested in fucking her. But getting her to suck my dick crossed my mind. I started to ask her to pull it out and lick on it. But she beat me to the punch.

"Let me give you some head," she said as she began to get down on her knees.

My dick was already hard. I didn't have to worry about getting erect. I sat and opened my legs a bit. Charlene unzipped my shorts and gently pulled my meat out. I had to admit that my shit was proudly standing at attention. She smiled at it and then she started talking to it. It was bugging me the fuck out.

"You want Mama to take care of you?" she began to say, and then she kissed the head of it. "I'm gonna make you feel real good."

She licked the tip of the head. Then she licked the head and slid my entire dick into her mouth. The pressure she put on my dick and the warmness of her mouth sent me over the edge. I was about to pull every strand of hair she had in her head, but I held my composure. I laid my head back against the headrest of the sofa. I closed my eyes a few times. When she did one of those tricks with her tongue to stimulate my dick, I opened my eyes to see what she was doing.

"Damn right, girl, suck this dick," I encouraged her. She seemed as if she was enjoying sucking my meat more than I was. She had my dick soaked. She even spit on the tip of it and then she licked it back off. This was a huge fucking turn-on.

I almost found myself wanting to fuck her pussy. That's just how good she was making my dick feel. But I snapped back to reality. I allowed her to suck my dick since that's technically not cheating. Bill Clinton did it and got away with it. I mean, if you look at it, I didn't plan on penetrating her and I didn't plan on kissing her, so I was in the clear. I didn't believe she would go back and tell Leon and Trice I let her give me some head. That would be stupid on her part. She would look like the ho. So I thought I was cool.

After twenty-two licks and sucks later, Charlene helped me explode right in her face. She massaged the shaft of my dick until the cum erupted from my dick. I saw her swallow some of it too. I smiled at her because she took me out of my element. I hadn't had my dick sucked in forever. She took me back to the days when I used to fuck with chicks that did all kinds of nasty shit for me. I wished Trice would serve me like Charlene just did. I believed our sex life would be much better.

Immediately after she drained me for every ounce of protein I had, she stood to her feet and began taking off her shorts, while I was stuffing my dick back into my shorts. Shocked by my actions, she asked me what I was doing.

"I'm getting ready to go into the bathroom and clean myself up," I replied, and then I stood up.

"What about me?" she asked. By this time she had taken off her shorts and her panties. She kept her bra and tank top on.

"Whatcha want me to do? I just came. I ain't got the energy to fuck you."

"You ain't gotta do anything. Just let me get on top of you. I can make myself come," she told me, and she sounded desperate. But I couldn't help her. My dick had gone limp and it would take an act of God to get it erect again. But who was I kidding? Even if my dick was able to get erect again, I wasn't going to play myself and stick my dick in her pussy. Her pussy belonged to Leon. They had a son together and that's where I drew the line.

"So you're telling me I'm ass out, huh?"

"Look, even if I did let you get on top of me, how are you going to get your rocks off when my dick ain't gon' be able to get hard?"

She sucked her teeth. "This is un-fucking-believable!" she snapped. Then she reached down to the floor and grabbed her panties and shorts. I walked by her and carried my ass to the bathroom to clean off. I knew she was furious with me, but I didn't care. I had no intention of fucking her from the beginning. She set herself up for this letdown. At the end of the day, she should blame herself.

While I was in the bathroom, I heard Charlene bitching in the other room. She was blowing off some steam, and it all had to do with me. "I know I did not let that motherfucker play me like that," I heard her venting. I stood there quietly and listened to her. "I can't believe he let me suck his dick and I get nothing in return. That's total bullshit!" she continued.

I listened to her rant on for at least three whole minutes until I figured it was time to shut her down. I knew it wasn't wise for her to be yelling throughout house. I couldn't let the microphones record her running her mouth. I walked into the living room where she was raising her voice and said, "Why are you in here fussing to yourself?"

"I just think it's fucked up how you played me," she answered.

"I didn't play you," I replied low enough for the recorder not to hear me.

"Then what do you call it?" she spat.

I walked closer to her. I needed to calm her down and get her emotions under control, so I leaned and placed my hand on her shoulder and did everything within my power to convince her that I was sorry. I also knew I had to blame my dick for not working either. But at the same time I knew I had to give her props for a job well done. Chicks loved it when a nigga told them how good their head game was. Chicks also liked it when niggas acted like we were exhausted after being fucked and sucked to death. "Do you realize how good you give head?" I started off saying. She sat there with a gullible expression on her face. I knew my tactic was working, so I kept going. "Charlene, I swear I've never had my dick sucked like that. Trice doesn't come close to you," I added.

Her frown slowly disappeared. She tried to keep her guard up, but I chipped away at it little by little. And it seemed to be working. "Hey, look, I promise that as soon as I build my stamina back up we'll get back down to business," I lied. I smiled at her in a way to reassure her that I was a man of my word.

She finally calmed her ass down after I lied to her a few more times. I figured this would buy me just a little more time. All I needed to do now was think of how I intended to blow her off completely. Sticking my dick inside of her wasn't an option for me.

That's Leon's pussy!

17

Trice

"Good morning, sleepy head," Leon said to me. I opened my eyes and saw him looking directly at me. He leaned over me as he sat alongside the bed. I slept in his bed last night and I had to admit, it felt good. My back felt well rested, but my heart sung a completely different song. I realized the alcohol had worn off, so reality reared its ugly face and reminded me about the night I had with Leon.

Every intricate detail ran through my mind and I began to feel really awful. The more I thought about what I had done, the worse my heart and stomach felt. But then I had to remind myself that I stepped out on my commitment to Troy because he left the door open for me after he stepped out on me with Charlene. I needed to rationalize the entire scenario so I could move forward without the guilt.

"Good morning," I replied, and then I rubbed my eyes. They were glassy from the sunlight beaming through the bedroom windows.

"Wanna go out for breakfast?" he asked me.

Without thinking much about it, I said, "Yes, sure."

"Well, get up and get dressed. I wanna take you to this place where they got some good breakfast."

I smiled. "Okay.

Leon pulled back the comforter and helped me out of bed. If it weren't for Leon's T-shirt and a pair of my panties, I would be naked. He smacked me on the butt when I stood on my feet. I giggled at his child's play because it was cute. I felt like a teenager sneaking around with her boy toy while my parents were out of town.

When I got into the bathroom, Leon already had my towel and bath cloth laid out for me. I hopped into the bathtub and took a hot shower. I couldn't believe it but Leon actually washed my back for me. In all the years I had been married to Troy, he never attempted to wash my back, even when we showered together. This was something new and even though it was a small gesture, I found it to be nice. Leon was generally a sweet guy. I thought he would try to get a quickie from me, but he remained a gentleman and kept his hands to himself.

After we both got dressed, we headed out to this breakfast café in Chesapeake. This was my first time at the eatery and I must admit, it had a nice Southern appeal to it. It was family owned and operated and they had superb hospitality. Leon and I both ordered the house special, which was a stack of pancakes, our choice of bacon or sausage, and two eggs cooked the way we wanted. We talked and laughed while we ate. And for some reason, it seemed as if we didn't run out of things to talk about. I really enjoyed myself.

Once Leon paid our check, we exited the restaurant, got back in his car, and headed to the oceanfront. Leon had this brilliant idea for us to go bike riding on the strip. Judging the book by its cover, I never would have imagined he would like to go out on an outing such as this. When I first met him, I'd bet every dime in my bank account that he was a street thug who sat in the house, puffed on a black and mild while he played Xbox 360. This side of Leon definitely caught me off guard.

During our bike ride, we ventured out on the beach area. We even rode the bikes on the busy strip. The whole scene was picture perfect. It was a happy ending to any story. And I enjoyed every minute of it.

When the bike ride ended, Leon and I got a cup of ice cream from Cold Stone and then we sat out on the beach. The scenery was beautiful, and I had good company to go along with it. I felt like I was in heaven. A couple of times Leon spoon-fed me some of his ice cream. I thought it was so sweet of him to do. And then I wondered why hadn't Troy ever done this for me? Small things meant more to me than any expensive vacation or a piece of jewelry.

"I am so glad Troy talked me into doing this wife-trading thing, because I am having the best time of my life."

I smiled. "So am I."

He smiled back at me. "So what do you want to do after this?"

"I'm not sure," I replied.

"Wanna go bungee jumping?" he asked me.

I was at a loss for words when he asked me if I wanted to go bungee jumping. I had always been afraid of heights. But the fact that he wanted to do something exciting gave me a warm feeling inside my heart. Unfortunately, I had to be realistic. I'd been afraid of climbing on anything over three stories high, so I had to decline his offer.

I did, however, think of something more adventurous for us to do. When I asked him if he wanted to go play miniature golf, he happily accepted. After we finished our ice cream, he grabbed me by the hand and escorted me down to the golf park. To all the strangers around us, we appeared to be newlyweds. But we knew differently. We also knew we had significant others who were spending time with each other, doing God knew what. On the surface it seemed like we didn't have a care in the world. But we knew better.

Leon expressed his discontent for Charlene. I tried to get him to say one thing good about her, but it didn't happen. I saw where he was going with this, and the sight of it wasn't pretty. At one point I empathized with him, which led me to express my feelings of betrayal concerning Troy. I could've gone on and on about Troy, but I decided against it. I figured I had talked about Troy enough. I learned growing up that a potential suitor doesn't want to hear about an ex-husband or ex-boyfriend. They figured if you've got a lot to say about them, then there's still some unresolved feelings lingering around, which wasn't a good look. And the best way to put that chapter of my life to bed was to leave well enough alone. In other words, I threw in the towel concerning Troy. I even made sure I kept my cell phone off, so Troy wouldn't be able to contact me.

In my heart and mind, I was over Troy.

18

Troy

Before I headed to work this morning, I got up and tried to get Trice on the phone again, but her voice mail picked up on the first ring. For the life of me, I couldn't figure out why she had her cell phone turned off. This was unlike her, and I began to get worried. I wanted to call Leon's cell phone, but I couldn't remember his number. Since I hadn't found my cell phone, I had no other choice but to wake Charlene up to get his number from her.

I entered my guest room with the cordless house phone in hand and repeatedly tapped Charlene on her shoulder until she woke up. After four taps she finally turned over and squinted as her eyes adjusted to the sunlight.

"I need Leon's cell phone number," I told her.

She turned and lay completely on her back. "What time is it?" she asked me.

"It's a few minutes after seven."

She paused for a couple of seconds and then she reached underneath the covers and grabbed her cell phone. After she flipped it open, she quickly closed it back. "Damn, I forgot to charge my phone last night," she finally said.

"I don't need to use it. I just want Leon's number," I told her.

"I know. But I can't get his number from my phone because it's completely dead."

Frustrated by her response, I said, "You don't know your own husband's number?"

"No. I don't. Because he just got his number changed two weeks ago. So I programmed it in my phone without trying to memorize it."

"Did you talk to him last night before you went to bed?"

"Nope. I ain't got shit to say to him," she barked.

"Well, can you charge your phone up so I can get his number before I leave for work?"

"I'm telling you right now that he ain't gonna answer his phone."

"He may not answer it for you, but I know he'll answer it for me," I assured her, and then I tapped her on the arm. "So can you get up and charge your phone right now?"

Charlene took her time, but she slid out of bed and searched for her charger. I left the bedroom and headed downstairs to the kitchen. I made myself a cup of hot tea while I waited for her to charge her phone.

Meanwhile, she joined me in the kitchen. She walked in wearing a white tank top and a pair of thong panties. Her panties hugged her pussy real tight, so it looked inviting. She had a three-inch gap between her thighs and that turned me on too. My dick was getting hard by the second. But I knew I couldn't fuck with her this morning. Therefore, I immediately took my focus off her and concentrated on stirring the sugar I had just added to my cup of tea.

"Cooking breakfast this morning?" she asked. Then she paraded herself around me. She walked to the refrigerator and opened the door. She stood there and acted as if she was looking for something. Hell, I knew better. She stood there so I could get a good view of her fat ass. I mean her ass was so big and soft-looking. Being a man, I thought about bending her ass over and fucking the shit out of her. I actually pictured sliding my dick into her pussy and fucking the shit out of her while I smacked the back of her ass cheeks. Boy, that sounded like fun. However, I quickly snapped back into reality. I allowed her to suck my dick the night before but I refused to take it farther than that. She seemed like one of those fatal attraction chicks who wanted to attach herself to me. Since I didn't need that headache, I answered her question by telling her I wasn't cooking breakfast and I turned my attention back to my cup of tea.

She grabbed a bottle of spring water from the refrigerator, took a swallow, and gave me this disappointed expression. "But I thought you were the host around here."

I gave her a fake-ass smile. "I got to be at work within the next hour, so the only thing I can do for you is make you a bowl of cereal," I told her as I sipped my tea.

"You know what I noticed about you?" she asked.

"What?"

"It seems like every time I want you to do something for me, you always find an excuse not to do it."

"It's not like that," I lied.

"Then how is it?" she pressed the issue as she took another swallow of water.

I took another sip of my hot tea. "You just catch me at bad times."

"So if I asked you to slide my panties to the side and fuck me right now, would you do it?"

I wanted to laugh in her face because she

caught me completely off guard with that question. One part of me wanted to tell her I wouldn't fuck her with her husband's dick, because she wasn't worth me losing my wife. But I held my tongue and acted like a gentleman.

"Look, Charlene, you're an attractive woman, and you got a banging-ass body, but I can't get down with you like that. I fought with myself for an hour trying to figure out if I should've given you the dick after you gave me head yesterday."

"I bet I can figure out the outcome of that," she commented sarcastically.

I tried to respond to her comment, but I couldn't. Her comment was funny as hell, but I couldn't bring myself to laugh in her face, so I gave her the serious face and convinced her that if things were different, we would've taken things to another level. Unfortunately for me, that excuse wasn't good enough.

"I don't think you got the memo. Because after I opened my mouth and sucked your dick last night, we took it to the next level."

"That was different."

"How the fuck was that different?"

"It's different because I didn't penetrate you," I tried to explain. Why I tried, I don't know. The more I talked, the more frustrated and angry she got. I dug a hole so deep for myself that it was impossible for me to ever recover from it. I was losing big-time.

Charlene was boiling on the inside. She was so fucking mad at me that she took two steps toward me and slammed her bottle of water on the countertop near me. "You know what, Troy? Fuck you! You're just like my no-good-ass husband. As a matter of fact, all y'all niggas are alike," she snapped. Her tone was full of venom.

"Can you please calm down?" I tried to reason.

"Calm down? Really, Troy?" Her voice got louder.

"Yes, let's talk about this like sensible adults."

"Oh, so now I'm not a sensible adult?" she continued to roar.

"Look, Charlene, I just want you to calm down so we can talk about this."

"What is there to talk about? I sucked your dick last night, you came, I didn't, and now you want me to listen to some random bullshit? Nigga, please, get out of my damn face before I get ghetto up in here."

"There's no need for you to get ghetto. So let's drop the whole conversation."

"Oh, so that's it? How fucking convenient!" she replied sarcastically, and then she snatched her bottle of water from the countertop and made her exit.

I watched her as she stormed out of the kitchen. Her ass shook from left to right. It even jiggled a little bit. She definitely had a fat ass, but that was it. She was a hood chick and she had the IQ of a fucking horse. Lucky for me, I only had to spend three more days with her silly ass. After that, she'll have to return to her husband and I'll be home free. So I say good riddance. *Take that fucked-up attitude back home to Leon. Let him put up with your shit. And send my wife back home.*

I sure take my hat off to Leon for putting up with Charlene all these years.

19

Charlene

I had to get away from that nigga Troy and go to the bedroom before I flipped out on his ass. How dare that bastard try to play me like he did? I'm not a fucking toy, and he needed to know that. He had me sucking his fucking dick like a champion and had the audacity not to want to fuck me after the fact. And to add insult to injury, that motherfucker had the balls to tell me he couldn't make me breakfast. What kind of bullshit was that? I was the guest of honor and he was supposed to be the host. What happened to hospitality? Was I missing something? What's his fucking problem?

"You think your phone has charged up enough so you can get Leon's number from it?"

I heard him yell from downstairs. Instead of answering him, I closed the bedroom door. I sat back down on the bed and waited for him to come upstairs behind me and ask me that question again so I could tell him to kiss my ass. He definitely barked up the wrong tree this morning. I don't play with niggas . . . especially ones that take me for granted.

He better ask my dumb-ass husband what I was capable of. I was a bitch when a nigga rubbed me the wrong way. I'd make you wish you'd never crossed my path. And before I left this house, he was gonna wish he'd never met me. I was going to tear his perfect little world apart. And his wife was going to be caught dead in the middle. *Watch and see.*

Five minutes passed and Troy climbed the flight of stairs and showed up at the bedroom door. He knocked four times and called my name, but I ignored him. So he took it upon himself to let himself into the room. I knew it would fuck with his head if I was naked when he walked in, so that's exactly what I did.

"Oh, I'm sorry," he said when he saw me, covering his eyes. He didn't leave the room, but he made sure he kept his eyes covered while he talked to me. "Do you think your phone is charged enough so that you can turn it on and get your husband's number?"

I rolled my eyes at him. "Nah, it's gonna take at least thirty minutes before it's charged up really good."

"Come on now, it doesn't take that long," he griped. He had become frustrated with my answer, because he took his hand from eyes and gave me this intense look. In my opinion, he looked like he wanted to choke my ass. So I braced myself and waited for him to make the first move.

"Charlene, I don't believe your phone gotta be charged for thirty minutes to get it to work," he continued as he rushed toward my phone. He was fixated on getting Leon's number so he could get in touch with his wife. But I wasn't having that. I wasn't about to let him go through my phone. That cell phone belonged to me. It was my personal property and he needed to respect that fact.

I grabbed my phone before he could get it. Since I was able to get to it before he could, he went to the extent of trying to take it from me.

"Girl, stop playing and give me that phone," he demanded.

I was shocked at how aggressive he had gotten over my damn cell phone. He wrestled me down to the bed while I was naked so he could take my phone from me. How fucking crazy was he? He had a lot of nerve.

"Can you get the fuck off me?" I asked. I was tired as hell of trying to prevent him from taking my phone out of my hand.

"Give me your phone and I'll get off you," he told me.

Still struggling to keep my phone in my hands, I managed to turn over onto my stomach. I buried the phone underneath me while he had me pinned to the bed.

"I am not going to give you my phone," I told him.

"Well, I'm not gonna get off you until you do."

"That's fine. I can lie in this position all day," I told him. Then I started grinding my butt on his dick. He tried desperately to block my advances, but he couldn't. His dick was getting hard by the second.

"Hmmm, I feel that dick of yours getting hard on my ass," I continued, and then I giggled.

"That ain't my dick."

I laughed aloud at his lie. "Come on, Troy. Stop fronting. You know you want this pussy."

"Charlene, give me your phone," he said, trying to dismiss my comment.

"I told you what you gotta do," I replied as I stuck to my guns. I wasn't about to give him my phone. If he gave me some of that big dick he had, then I would consider giving him my cell phone. Other than that, he didn't have a thing coming.

He hesitated for a moment, and then he said, "A'ight. You win. I'll give you some of this dick. But as soon as I push this meat up inside of you I want you to hand me the phone."

After he agreed to give me a quick fuck, I rested my breasts on my hands to secure my phone and then I got on my knees and poked out my butt to give him easy access. I looked back at him while he unbuttoned his work pants. Within seconds, he had his big, erect dick in his hand, ready to go for what he knew. I was so ready for him to give me everything he had.

"You ready for this dick?" he asked me as he stood alongside the bed. Before I could answer him, he smacked me on the butt cheeks with the head of his dick. I watched as his dick bounced back off my ass every time he popped it.

"Whatcha waiting for? Stick it in this wet pussy!" I whined. I swear, my pussy was leaking with juices. I wanted him like there was no to-morrow.

"Turn around and lick on it first," he de-manded.

I hesitated at first because I was only ready for him to fuck my brains out. I wasn't in the mood to suck his dick. I had already done it the night before. But then I figured it would be a win-win situation if I got him more aroused. A couple of licks would get his dick so hard, he wouldn't have a choice but to fuck me to death.

Like the down-ass chick I was, I got up from my knees and turned around toward Troy with my cell phone gripped tightly in my left hand. With my right hand I grabbed his dick and leaned in toward it. As soon as I pushed the top half of his penis into my mouth, he reached underneath my chin and tried to snatch the phone away from me. Too bad for him I saw him coming long before he made his move.

I immediately took his dick from my mouth and jumped back. When I did that, he pushed me onto my back, but I was able to keep him from taking the phone from me. I placed both of my hands behind my back. Troy wrestled with me to get my hands from behind my back.

"Stop playing and give me your damn phone," he grunted.

To get him away from me, I managed to kick him in the stomach. I was aiming for his dick since it was hanging out of his pants, but he blocked me. After we wrestled for a few more seconds, he got tired and let me go. He huffed and puffed as he crawled off me.

"Man, fuck it! I ain't got time for this shit," he complained as he climbed off the bed. When he stood back on his feet, he pushed his dick into his pants and zipped up his pants.

I sat there on the bed and watched him as he whined about not being about to get my cell phone away from me. I cracked a smile at him and told him how I felt about his little game.

"When you play childish games, you get treated like a child," I commented. I became angrier than ever before.

I thought Troy would reply to my comment, but he didn't. Instead, he walked out of the bedroom without saying another word. And when he shut the door behind himself, I lay there and reflected on how he promised to fuck me and reneged on me once again. I felt violated all over again. I even felt like a cheap hooker. Troy sure knew how to play with my self-worth. I knew I was Leon's wife, but I was still a woman and I deserved a little respect. But unfortunately, that asshole lacked in that area. Too bad I had an advantage over him, that being his cell phone.

I vowed to make sure his fucking cell phone disappeared forever.

20

Leon

Trice and I hung out all day at the beach, and I could definitely say we enjoyed each other's company. We headed back to my place around four o'clock that afternoon. As soon as we stepped through my front door, we laid it down. She got her a spot on one end of my sofa and I sat my ass in my recliner and leaned the chair back as far as I could. Before I got good and comfortable, I turned on the TV and flipped to an old *Sanford and Son* rerun. By the time the show was halfway over, Trice was sound asleep.

I found myself staring at her during the commercial breaks. She looked so peaceful and I found her more beautiful than ever. I even went to the extent of getting out of my chair to kiss her on the forehead. When I sat back down in my chair, I stared at her some more. The question of why couldn't she have been my wife kept circling my mind. I believed if she were my wife instead of Troy's, then I would be a happier man. She possessed all the qualities I looked for in a woman. She smelled good. She was classy and was funny. Plus, her pussy was good. I could also tell she was a clean freak, which was what I loved the most.

Charlene was one nasty bitch. She would leave the bathroom tub dirty for at least five straight days before she got off her ass and cleaned it. She'd also leave the kitchen sink filled with dirty dishes for two to three days. I hate washing dishes. So I had to curse her out for an hour before she'd get in there and handled her business.

I still couldn't believe Charlene cleaned the whole house before she left our house to go to Troy's crib. When I came home from work and saw her busting the suds in the kitchen sink, I asked if she was feeling all right. Of course, I can't remember what she said, but I was sure it was something slick that came out of her mouth. I shook my head and she went on about her business.

While I daydreamed about the ifs, ands, and buts, it dawned on me that I hadn't heard my cell phone ring for quite some time. I remembered turning the power off last night after I talked to Charlene and never turned it back on. When I pressed the power button, the screen lit up instantly. I looked at the LCD screen and noticed I had five voice mails and ten text messages. There was no doubt in my mind that all those messages came from Charlene. I wasn't in the right frame of mind to listen to the voice mails, so I strolled down the menu bar and pulled up her text messages. I braced myself for every nasty word I was about to read, because our last conversation ended on a bad note.

Nigga u so funny it's pathetic! U always act like I'm da one who fucked up our marriage, the first message read.

U fucked it up a long time ago when u fucked dat bitch, the second message read.

The third text read, *U doin' me a fava by tellin me it's over. Fuck u! I can do betta!*

Afta all dis is ova I'm taking my half of da $ & I'm leavin'. So kiss my ass! BITCH!

After I read the last message, I pressed the red exit button. I realized I had read enough. There was no need to continue feeding into her bullshit. She and I both knew what time it was. Our marriage was over a long time ago. But since she said she's leaving, I was going to let her ass go. And later in life when my son came to me and asked me why we divorced, I was going to tell him his mother left me. And that would be the end of that.

Right after I exited the text message application, I stuck my phone down into my front pocket and watched Trice as she lay there before me. I was mesmerized at how I was drawn to her. I stared at her flawless features and I started thinking of the possibilities of *her and me* becoming an *us* . . . being together after she divorced Troy. The thought of her being in my life made me feel good. I would be so happy if I woke up to her beautiful face every morning. Now, I knew Troy wouldn't be in favor of this, and I knew this would fuck up our friendship, but hey, I figured what's good for him was good for me. I mean, it ain't like he hadn't fucked my wife. He and Charlene opened that door way before Trice and I did. So I was sure he'd get over it one day.

I could see it now. Trice and I could be like Will and Jada Pinkett Smith, without all the money. I could see her as my partner because she was a genuine sweetheart. I saw no malice in her heart at all. And the fact that we had a lot of things in common gave me the best feeling ever. There was no doubt that she was my soul mate. I could honestly see myself not fucking around on her either. She was the type of chick a nigga would be a fool to mess up with. I swear, I was counting down the days until all of this was over and she broke the news to Troy. Boy, I was going to be sitting on top of the world . . . of course with Trice at my side.

Once I felt like I had stared at her long enough, I got up from my chair. I suddenly had a certain urge for a beer. I didn't have any cold ones in my refrigerator, so I had to head out to the local corner store to get some. Before I left the house, I tapped Trice on her arm and told her I was about to go to the store. After she opened her eyes, I asked her if she wanted something while I was out. She told me no.

"Well, if you think of something while I'm out, call me," I told her, and then I left.

On my way to the store, I couldn't stop thinking about Trice.

I think I'm in love!

21

Troy

On my way home from work I began thinking about how I hadn't spoken to Trice in the last couple of days. I thought about wrecking shop a few times. The fact that Charlene's dumb ass wouldn't give me Leon's number sent me over the edge. I was really close to telling that bitch to get the fuck out of my crib. But I kept cool. I only had a couple more days with this cunt and then she'd be gone for good, back at her own house driving her husband crazy.

When I merged onto Highway 264, I began to drive the entire seven miles to get to my exit, but I had a sudden urge to make a detour and stop off in Norfolk. So that's what I did.

The idea of going by Leon's place fueled my

adrenaline. It gave me an energy blast I hadn't felt in a while. All I wanted to do was see Trice. I didn't have to talk to her. I just wanted to get one good look at her, just to make sure she was all right. And once I accomplished that mission, I promised I would leave immediately thereafter. I knew she wanted me to have the ten-thousand-dollar cash prize as much as I did, so I knew I couldn't jeopardize losing it.

Right after I arrived in Leon's neighborhood, I slowed my truck and cruised down every street until I arrived on the block where he resided. My heart immediately started beating uncontrollably. It was a combination of me trying not to get caught and wanting desperately to see Trice's face. But as soon as I came within two hundred feet of his house, I noticed his car was nowhere in sight and I instantly became angry. I looked down at my watch and saw that it was a few minutes after seven o'clock, so where in the hell could they be? And since I didn't have the answers to my questions, I decided to pull my truck over and park it at a safe distance from his house. I figured if I waited around for a few minutes, then they'd probably show up.

Meanwhile, as I sat in my truck, I realized how frequently police officers patrolled this neighborhood. This part of Norfolk wasn't as hood as the other parts of the city, but it wasn't the nicest. Leon was considered a blue-collar worker. His wife, Charlene, was borderline Section 8 and hood fabulous. Hell, if I called her that, she would take it as a compliment.

I remember the day they met. Charlene looked a lot better back then, and she had a little bit more class than she did now. I think she switched up on my boy when she started hanging out at Upscale's nightclub every Thursday, Friday, and Saturday night. Leon used to complain about it, but it didn't work. She had the attitude that she could do anything she wanted. So when she popped up pregnant, Leon refused to believe the baby was his until she gave him a paternity test. When the results came back, Leon was proven to be the father, which meant he was stuck with her forever.

I couldn't imagine the drama, especially when it came to childbirth. The birth of a child was supposed to be golden between married couples, not drama-filled on who was the father.

I thought their relationship would turn around, but it didn't. And the way things look now, I didn't think their situation would ever work out. I did know that I wouldn't let their drama affect my marriage. I would die before I let their mess filter over into my household. Hell no! I wouldn't let that shit happen for all the money in the world.

After I ran down all the wrong decisions Leon and Charlene made, I saw the Dodge Magnum headlights coming up behind me. Once the car got within five feet of my truck, I knew it was Leon behind the wheel. I immediately readjusted my eyes to look in my rearview mirror to see if I saw Trice in the passenger seat, but I couldn't because it was too dark. So I waited for the car to pass me and when it did, I fixed my eyes on the passenger side. I knew that I would be able to get a better look from that angle. When the car came alongside my truck, I looked straight into the passenger side window and my heart sank in the pit of my stomach when I didn't see my wife.

She was nowhere to be seen. That's when I knew she had to be inside his house. I waited for Leon to park his car and then I called him over to my truck. He had this weird look on his face as he approached me.

"What's up?" he said while he tried to manage three grocery bags in his hands.

I tried to play it cool. I didn't want him to think I was sweating him and Trice. So I reached outside my truck and gave him the proper handshake. "Everything's good?" I started off. "What's going on?" I asked him.

"Nothing. I just ran off to the store to get a few things for the house. Trice didn't wanna come. We hung out at the beach all day, so she's in the house taking a nap."

"Oh, so she's in the house?"

Leon took a look at his surroundings and then he looked back at me. "Yeah, she's probably still asleep too," he finally said. Then he came back at me and said, "You know if you get caught around here, those people aren't gonna give you and Trice that ten grand."

"I know. But I had to stop over here since I hadn't heard from her. I've been trying to call her cell phone for the past couple of days and all I get is her voice mail."

Leon took another look at our surroundings. "You know I love you like a brother, but I ain't gonna be able to help you if those people catch you snooping around here."

"I know. I know. I'm just all fucked up in the head 'cause I ain't talked to Trice. And what's really fucked up is the fact that I lost my phone in the process."

Leon shook his head. "If you got a GPS tracker on it, you'll be able to find it."

"Nah, I don't have a GPS tracker on my phone. And I can kick myself in the ass for it, too, because I declined that service when I renewed my service plan a couple months ago."

"Sounds like you're fucked!"

"Yeah, I know," I replied. "But do me a favor."

"Sure. What's up?"

"Have Trice call me."

"I thought you said you lost your cell phone?"

"I did. I want her to call the house phone."

Leon turned around to take a quick look at his house and then he looked back at me. "Want me to tell her to call you if she's up?" he asked me.

"Yeah," I replied.

"Okay, I can do that," he told me, and then he slapped me some dap as if to say he was about to make his exit. But I wasn't about to let that nigga leave without giving me his cell phone number.

"Hey, Leon, what's your cell phone number again?" I asked him.

He acted as if I had caught him off guard. He stood there like he had to think about it before he gave it to me. Then after thirty seconds, the numbers finally rolled off his lips. He said it so fast I had to ask him to repeat it. Immediately after he gave me his cell phone number for the second time, he reminded me not to let the execs from the show see me in the area.

I took his lame-ass excuse of encouraging me to get out of there with a grain of salt while I watched him walk away from my truck. When he disappeared into the house, I pulled back onto the road ahead of me. As I drove away from his neighborhood, I thought to myself how weird that nigga acted. As long as I've known him, he's never acted standoffish like he did a few minutes ago. I noticed how he tried to blame his behavior on the money we're supposed to get, but my gut was telling me something wasn't right.

* * *

When I got back to my house, Charlene was in the kitchen eating Chinese food she ordered. I gave her the biggest smile I could muster up and said hello. She looked at me like I was crazy before she spoke back to me. I could tell she wasn't in the mood to talk to me because of what happened earlier, but it didn't matter to me. I was going to get what I wanted to say off my chest.

"Has Trice tried to call the house phone while I was gone?" I asked her. I needed to make sure I hadn't missed my wife's phone call.

"Nope. The house phone hasn't rung at all."

"Guess who I saw today?"

"I really don't care," she answered between chews.

"Well I'm gonna tell you anyway." I smirked.

Charlene gave me the evil eye.

"I saw Leon," I told her as I stood three feet away from her.

She stopped chewing her food. "So what?" she spat.

I threw my hands up. "Damn! Don't bite my head off."

"I ain't gonna touch you. But at the same time, I don't wanna hear shit about that trifling-ass nigga. I'm sitting here enjoying my food and that's how I would like to be."

"A'ight. No problem," I replied, and turned to leave the kitchen. But then I thought to myself that I couldn't let her off that easy. She made it perfectly known that she was tired of her husband as well as me and that she couldn't wait to get away from us all. So I had to make mention of that. I stopped in my tracks and turned back around.

"I know you're glad you only have two more days left to be here."

"Trust me, I'm counting down the minutes," she replied, and then she rolled her eyes at me and put her attention back on her food.

I smiled and shook my head because I could see how miserable she was and believe it or not, it tickled me to death. I swear I was so proud of myself for not sticking my dick in her. That chick was insane. I had always known that if you fuck women who are not emotionally stable, they will ruin a man's life. Boy, did I make a good judgment call with that or what?

I badgered her for every bit of twenty minutes and then I headed to my bedroom. I crawled onto my bed after I closed my bedroom door. I picked up the cordless phone from the lamp stand near my bed just to make sure the ringer was on. I even scrolled down the call log on the phone just to make sure Charlene hadn't lied about Trice calling me. If I found out otherwise, she'd have to leave my fucking house tonight. Luckily for her, I didn't see where Trice could've called me.

I set the cordless phone back on the base and then used the remote control to turn on the TV. I sifted through the channels to find something interesting to watch. After I realized there was nothing on worth watching, I decided to watch the news. With all the bullshit going on around the Tidewater area, there was plenty of news to look and listen to.

Fifteen minutes into the broadcast, I noticed that Trice still hadn't picked up her phone to call me. I wasn't too happy about that. I figured that something was not right. And the way Leon acted when I saw him kind of confirmed that he was holding back from me. He and I were close friends, so why was he acting so fucking strange? Was he hiding something from me? And if so, what was it? I certainly hoped that it wasn't the affair that Charlene had alleged happened. Boy, that would be a hard pill to swallow if it was. The thought of it alone made me sick to my stomach. So the best thing for me to do right now was to toss that thought out of my head and focus on the future with Trice. I can honestly say that this experience with Charlene made me appreciate my wife more. And right now would be a good time to call Leon's cell phone so that I could talk to her and tell her how much I loved and missed her.

I will never mistreat her again.

22

Trice

Leon woke me up with a kiss on my forehead. I opened my eyes and he gave me the biggest smile ever. He was such a gentleman. I turned around on the sofa and lay on my back so I could get a full view of him. He took a seat on the edge of the sofa next to me. We were side by side.

"I just saw Troy," he told me.

My heart dropped after he mentioned that he'd seen my husband. "Where?" I asked. Anxiety crept in that moment.

"He was inside his truck just outside the house, but he was parked on the opposite side of the street."

"You're kidding, right?"

"No, I'm not. And when I got out of my car, I walked over to talk to him."

The thought of Troy coming within yards of the house made me feel uneasy, especially with everything that had happened between Leon and I. So I sat up that instant. "What did he say?" I asked.

"He wanted to know where you were."

"What did you tell 'im?"

"I told him that you were in the house. And that you were probably asleep because we had been out all day."

"And what did he say?"

"He said that he needed to come 'round here and check on you to make sure that you were all right because he hadn't talked to you in a couple days."

"Did you tell him that I was fine and that you were taking good care of me?" I replied sarcastically. I was getting very irritated by all the questions Troy had had for Leon. He needed to be more concerned about Charlene because I was in a good space. The time I'd spent with Leon was worth my sanity. Now I wished that I'd cheated on Troy long before yesterday.

"Nah, it wasn't my place to say that. I did assure him that you were good."

"How did you get rid of him?"

"I told him that it would be a bad idea to get caught being around here. So, he listened to me. But before he left he told me to tell you to give him a call. And to call him on the house phone because he somehow lost his cell phone."

I sucked my teeth. I mean, how dare that bastard ask me to call him after what Charlene told me? Was he on drugs or something? "I'm not calling him," I finally said.

"I kind of figured you wouldn't. But I didn't tell him that," Leon added.

"Well, did you tell him that you knew he fucked your wife?"

"No, I didn't."

"Did he tell you that he fucked your wife?" I wanted to know.

"No. I didn't mention it. I thought he was going to say something about it. But he acted like nothing went on between them."

I rolled my eyes. I was upset at the fact that Troy would have the audacity to come around here and show his face after all that shit that went on with him and Charlene. And then to ask Leon to have me call him was like a slap in the face. I mean, what kind of fool did he think I was? I knew one thing: He could lie all he wanted about what went on between him and Charlene, because at this point I didn't care. I was going to move on with my life and he wouldn't be a part of it.

After Leon and I completed our talk about Troy and Charlene, we got up and went into the kitchen. He showed me the items he brought back from the grocery store and then he sat me down at the table while he prepared dinner. I laughed the entire time he paraded around the kitchen because he had a joke for everything. Before I realized it, I had taken my mind off Troy—that is, until Leon's cell phone rang.

Leon looked at me immediately after he looked at the caller ID. I started to tell him not to answer it, but something inside of me told me to keep my mouth closed.

"You know he's calling to talk to you," he said to me.

"Well, I really don't want to talk to him," I replied.

"You know if you don't answer this call, he's going to come back over here," Leon replied, and then he held out the phone for me to grab it.

Before I took it, I thought about how I was going to act after I said hello. I knew I didn't want to start a big commotion, so I figured if I played his game and acted as if everything was okay, then he'd get back the same medicine he dished out to Leon earlier. So when it seemed as if the phone was about to stop ringing, I took it and pressed the SEND button.

I tried to say hello, but the words wouldn't come out of my mouth. Troy knew that someone had answered the phone, because he said hello before I could. After I quietly cleared my throat, I finally was able to say hello as well.

He sounded like he was really happy to hear my voice. But I knew it was all out of guilt. So I said fuck it and played along with his stupid-ass game. "Hey what's up?" I responded nonchalantly.

"Nothing much. I've just been worried about you."

"Don't worry about me. I'm fine."

"Well, it's hard not to worry when I've been trying to call your cell phone and it keeps going straight to the voice mail. What's wrong with it?"

"My battery is dead," I lied.

"Where is your phone charger?"

"I don't know. I misplaced it somewhere," I continued to lie.

"Why didn't you call and tell me that?"

"Because I've been busy."

"Busy doing what?"

"What's with all the questions?" I asked him. I was becoming very annoyed. I didn't think that he had the right to question me the way he was doing.

"So I can't ask you questions now?"

"I'm not saying you can't ask me questions."

"Well what are you saying?"

"Look, Troy, I am not trying to argue with you. I've had a long day."

"I'm not trying to argue with you either. I just want to know what's going on with you. And is there something you're not telling me?"

"There is nothing going on. So, can we please talk about something else?"

"Are you sure?" he pressed the issue.

I sucked my teeth. "Yes, I am sure," I responded. I was becoming more and more bothered by the constant questions. I felt he had serious nerve asking me a ton of questions when he was the one who couldn't keep his dick in his pants to begin with. I was on the verge of cursing his ass out, but when I looked at Leon, he placed his hand over his mouth, giving me the signal not to go any further with this conversation. It was quite obvious to Leon and I that Troy was trying to get me to confess to something.

"Well, I don't believe it. You telling me that you misplaced your cell phone charger and that you've been too busy to call and tell me just doesn't sit well with me. I've been married to you long enough to know when something isn't right with you. And right now is one of those times."

"Well, Troy, you're wrong. I am fine."

"That's bullshit, Trice, and you know it," he roared. He sounded as if he was about to lose it and snap out on me. But I defused the situation quickly. I didn't want any drama right now while we were being taped for the show. I wanted this whole thing to be over with before I broke the news to him that I was filing for divorce. So before I answered his question, I took a deep breath and said, "Look, Troy, I told you once before that I am not in the mood to argue with you right now. So can we please drop it?"

"Yeah, we can drop it after you tell me what's going on."

"There's nothing going on. Now, are you satisfied?"

"Nah, I'm not satisfied because I know you're lying."

"How dare you call me a liar when you're the one who's always gotten caught telling me lies in the past. I have put up with a lot of your bullshit for years. And now you come at me with an assumption because you're feeling guilty about something you've done. You better check yourself before I check it for you!" I snapped back.

I thought he would come back at me with another fireball to continue with our heated argument. Troy was the type of man who'd die to stay in control. He always had to have the last word, but he proved me wrong and didn't utter another word. He and I sat and listened to each other breathe into the phone for at least a minute before we were interrupted by Charlene's voice in the background.

"Are you okay?" I heard her ask him.

"Why the fuck are you bothering me right

now?" I heard him snap at her. "I am on the phone trying to have a private conversation with my wife, so can you please leave me alone?" Then he said, "Hello, Trice, you still there?"

Before I answered him, I thought about how quickly he snapped on her. It didn't sound like the match-made-in-heaven relationship she bragged about. So at that point I had every intention of asking him what happened between them. However, Leon was in my face, so I decided not to open up that can of worms. I did acknowledge that I was still on the line and told him I had to go. He didn't like that answer too well and tried everything in his power to keep me on the phone.

"Look, baby, I'm sorry if I upset up. But you see, I haven't been able to talk to you in the past couple of days and that wasn't sitting right with me. It had me thinking that some foul shit was going on. And you know when I start thinking crazy I won't let it go until I get some answers."

"Yeah, I know," I finally responded.

"So are we straight?"

"Yeah, we straight," I lied. I told him what he wanted to hear because I was ready to get off the phone.

"A'ight. Well, call me before you go to bed tonight. And call the house phone because I misplaced my cell phone."

"All right."

"I love you."

"I love you too," I replied, and almost bit my fucking tongue off doing it. I was really upset with his ass, so how was I going to say *I love you* back without having mixed feelings? Whether my husband knew it or not, his time with me was coming to an end. And it was a travesty that he didn't see it coming.

After I hung up with Troy, Leon came over and embraced me and told me I handled Troy really well. I didn't know if he was sincere or not, but after he sealed his comment with a kiss on my forehead, I had no choice but to believe him.

Looks like I'm Team Leon!

23

Charlene

I couldn't believe I let that nigga play me like that while he was screaming at his wife on the fucking phone. Shit, I was only trying to see if his dumb ass was all right. And this was the thanks I got? Fuck him and her! He was lucky I didn't curse his ass out. I mean, who the fuck did he think he was trying to show off in front of his wife? That bitch couldn't hold a candle to me, so he had better get his motherfucking act together before I fucked his relationship up worse than it was. Leon should've warned that dummy that I wasn't the bitch to fuck with. I was the most scandalous person that walked the face of the earth. I would make a nigga's life so miserable he'd think I had roots on his ass.

Right after I left him, I went and took me a hot shower. I needed to clear my mind and come up with an exit strategy from my no-good-ass husband. He and I both knew that we had come to the end of our rope. The thing that lingered in my mind was that I hadn't thought about where I would go after we separated. I had to figure out who was going to live in the house. But knowing Leon, he'd want his son and I to stay there while he ran off and found somewhere else to live. I believe that if we didn't have a son together, he'd put me out in the street in a heartbeat.

The one thing that concerned me most was how he was going to act when it was time to divvy up the ten grand. I knew there was going to be some problems with him splitting the money down the middle. He always felt like he was the overall breadwinner since he paid the majority of the bills, so he may want the majority of the money. But being that we're going to separate, that changes the game. I tell you what! I wouldn't sign that check unless I was getting my half. Fuck that! With all of that motherfucker's bullshit I had put up with, I deserved to get what was due to me. And I was gonna get it. Or he could kiss that money good-bye, because neither one of us would see it. And that was my final word.

I believed I stayed in the shower for thirty minutes and when the water started turning cold, I shut it off and got out. I wrapped a towel around me and headed back to the bedroom I had been sleeping in. I had a strong mind to lose the towel and parade around Troy naked, but then I figured it would be a waste of time. He'd act like he didn't see me or even worse, he'd tell me to get out of his face and go put some fucking clothes on as if I looked disgusting or something. He was definitely a class-A asshole. And he was a tough cookie to crack. But I hadn't given up the fight yet. I was going to get my just do before the ink dried on the checks. Just wait and see.

After I slipped on my nightclothes, I started packing up my things for the day I left this damn house. I had less than forty-eight hours and I couldn't wait.

Lights. Camera. Action.

24

Leon

After Troy called my cell phone to talk to Trice that first time, he called at least three times after that. To keep the drama down, she called him once, but she didn't stay on the phone long. I believed the reason she didn't talk long was because she knew I was listening to their conversation. I also knew it was only a matter of time before the shit hit the fan, but I was ready to go head-to-head with Troy to let him know where I stood with Trice. I wasn't sure whether he would get physical with me, but I was ready to go for what I knew. I mean, as long as Trice stuck to her guns and professed her love for me, I had to be the man in the situation and have her back. As I thought about what could go on from this point, I watched Trice as she packed up her things to leave the house. She only had one more night to be here and then she had to go.

"Think I can get me some of that good loving before you leave?" I asked her, and then I smiled.

She smiled back at me as she placed folded shirts into her luggage. "Didn't I just give you some this morning when you woke up with a hard-on?"

I walked up behind her and placed my arms around her waist. I thrust my dick against her soft, fat ass as I pressed my lips against her neck. "You know I can't get enough of you," I told her.

She continued to fold and place her things into her bag. "You're not falling in love with me already, are you?"

I hesitated for a second because I really didn't know how to answer that question. I wanted to shout out to the world and tell her yes. But then I figured that would be the wrong move considering she hadn't told me how she really felt about me. I mean, she told me she loved being around me and that she could see herself with me, but the words *I love you* never came out of her mouth. So what was a brother to do?

And as I pondered on an answer, she said, "Don't tell me you're scared to tell me how you feel about me?"

Hearing her come back at me so quickly got me on the defense. "Look, I'm a grown-ass man. I'm not afraid of telling you how I feel."

"Well, answer the question," she pressed the issue.

I hesitated some more. "Yeah, I feel love in my heart for you."

She looked back at me and said, "That's good to know."

I was shocked by her answer. I honestly wanted to hear her tell me she loved me back. So I paused for a second and then I said, "Is that it? That's all you got to say?"

She gave me another one of her irresistible smiles and said, "It's not good for a woman to tell a man how she feels because he'll take it and run with it."

"And who told you that crap?" I asked her.

She started folding her things again. "It's a known fact."

"Says who?"

She turned her face toward me and kissed me on the cheek. "Don't get all worked up over nothing. All you need to know is that I have strong feelings for you and as long as you do right by me, we're going to be all right."

"Strong feelings, huh?"

"Yep."

"Well, you better do right by me too. Because I got a lot at stake."

"And I don't?" she replied.

"I didn't say that you didn't. All I'm saying is that, if we're gonna continue to see each other, we're gonna have to be straight up about everything and we can't let our exes come between us."

"You're not going to have any problems with Troy once I tell him what's up. And what about your wife? Don't you think she's gonna flip out once she gets the memo?"

"Remember, she started this shit!"

"Yeah, I know. But it doesn't change the fact that she's gonna take you through some baby mama drama."

"Nah, trust me. That ain't gon' happen."

She sucked her teeth. "Yeah, we'll see."

"You're right. We shall see."

I left the room so that Trice could finish packing her things. I told her to meet me in my bedroom when she was done. While I waited for her to come join me, I couldn't stop thinking about how I was going to act once she returned home to Troy. Was she going to tell him about our affair? Was she going to tell him that she's leaving him for me? And if she did tell him, would she follow through with it? Women were so unpredictable, so I found it hard that she'd go through anything dealing with change. I just hoped that whatever she decided to do, it involved me. I don't believe that I'm going to be able to live without her.

Aside from the decisions Trice had to make, I had to make a few of my own. I knew it was over with Charlene and I. But I couldn't figure out how I was going to cut my ties with her. Things would definitely get complicated because we had a son together. I've talked to so many niggas who broke off their relationship with their wife or baby mama and the chicks took them through hell. I can see it now. Charlene was the type of bitch who would try to keep my son away from me just to get underneath my fucking skin. She was really grimy. Not to mention, she'd keep me in court trying to eat me alive with child support payments. Phone calls with my son would be few and far between. And she'd make every excuse in the world that her actions are in the best interest of our child. Talk about a bullshit artist!

She'd make my life a living hell.

25

Troy

I was so fucking happy that today had finally come. Within the next hour, I was going to be reunited with my wife. I had already planned a nice day out for us. I knew she would be thrilled, especially when she found out that I was taking her to her favorite restaurant. And then afterward, I had planned to bathe her in a hot bubble bath. My goal today was to get our relationship back on track so we could move forward with our life. And instead of me paying a few things off with the ten thousand dollars, I was going to take Trice on the honeymoon she never had when we first got married. After all, she deserved it.

I raced around the house making sure everything was back in its proper place before I left to go and pick her up. I heard Charlene rambling around in the guest room getting dressed so we could leave. I had to admit that it was like music to my ears. In the beginning it was cool having her in my house, but when I saw how much of a con artist she was, I knew she was going to be a problem. I would say I got a nice dick suck out of the deal, but other than that she was a fucking headache and I was glad her time here had come to an end. After I straightened the pillows up on the sofa in the TV room, I yelled upstairs and asked Charlene if she was ready to hit the road.

"I'll be down in a minute," she replied.

"Yeah, a'ight," I said as I waited at the bottom of the staircase. I wanted us to walk out the house at the same time. After my cell phone disappeared, my gut told me she had something to do with it. There was no way in the world my phone had gotten up and walked out of the house. I'd never had problems with losing any of my other phones. Now all of a sudden I couldn't find a phone that I had just purchased a little over a month ago. I knew one thing, if I ever found out that bitch had my shit, I was going to make sure she paid for it in every way possible.

Finally, after I waited ten minutes, Charlene appeared at the top of the staircase with her bags in hand. She looked at me like she wanted me to help bring her things downstairs, but I dismissed her expression and walked toward the front door. After I opened the door so we could leave, she sucked her teeth and proceeded to drag her things down the stairs. She huffed and puffed until she reached the bottom step. Then she rolled her eyes as she dragged her bag past me.

"You could've helped me bring my bags downstairs. I mean, that's what any gentleman would've done," she commented as she headed toward the truck.

I started to make reference to her comment, but I figured it'd be a waste of my time and energy, so I ignored her dumb ass, locked my front door, and followed her to my truck. I was in a good mood because I was about to see Trice. There was no way I was going to let this ghetto bunny ruin a damn thing for me. Fuck that! Her miserable ass had to go back to where she belonged and I couldn't wait to get her there.

The entire drive to Norfolk took me less than fifteen minutes because I put the pedal to the metal. I felt as if I couldn't get Charlene home to Leon fast enough. It was time for us to do the switcheroo again. I was delivering his wife back to him. So he needed to give me my wife back. When I pulled up in front of his place, I didn't hesitate to blow my horn. I wanted Trice to hear my truck horn without any problems.

"Need help taking your bags in the house?" I asked Charlene. I knew she probably thought I had bumped my head, being as though I didn't help her take her things out of my house. But this time it was different. Trice was inside her house, so I figured if I helped Charlene take her things into her house, I could help Trice bring her things out to my truck and we could leave immediately after that.

"Nope, I don't need your help!" she snapped. Without saying another word, she snatched her bags from the backseat of my truck and dragged them up the sidewalk toward her house. I hopped out of the truck behind her and followed her to the front door. It didn't bother me that she didn't want me to help her with her bags. My main priority was Trice. So as soon as she stepped foot through the front door, everything else went out the window.

I watched Charlene as she entered the house. I started to follow her inside, but I figured that as soon as Trice saw her she'd know that I was outside and would come out to meet me. After Charlene walked inside, I walked up the steps and waited by the front door. Two minutes later, the door opened and out came Leon. I smiled at him and gave him a handshake. "What's good?" I asked him.

He stepped out on the porch area and closed the front door behind him. "I'm good. But I know shit around here is about to fall apart," he commented.

I knew he was referring to Charlene. She was definitely a major drama queen. But that was his mess, not mine. I really didn't care to talk about her. I was more interested in the whereabouts of my wife. I laughed and then I asked him if he knew if Trice was ready to go or not.

"She's already gone," he told me.

I was shocked. "What do you mean she's already gone?" I asked him.

"She left out of here in a cab about forty-five minutes ago," he replied. "I thought you knew."

"Hell nah, I didn't know. I was under the impression that when I dropped your wife off, I would be picking her up."

Leon gave me the dumbest expression he could muster up. "Yo, Troy, I swear I thought I heard her telling you she was going to take a cab home."

"When was this?"

"About an hour before she left."

"I don't know who the fuck she could've been talking to because it sure wasn't me. The last time I spoke to Trice was early this morning."

"Well, I don't know who she could've been talking to either. All I know is that she told someone she was catching a cab home. And then a few minutes later, she called a cab."

I was disgusted to no end hearing this punk-ass nigga tell me my wife left his crib in a fucking cab. What kind of bitch-ass move was that? I didn't let his stinking-ass wife come home in a cab, so why did he let my wife do it? I had every intention to flip out on this buster-ass nigga. I even wanted to question him about whether or not he fucked Trice, but I left well enough alone and bailed on his retarded ass. I didn't say good-bye when I bounced off his porch.

I jumped back in my truck with a big ball of emotions. I couldn't quite figure out what was going on in Trice's head for her to catch a cab to our house instead of waiting for me to pick her up. Her behavior had gotten so odd I could no longer figure her out.

I wished I had my fucking cell phone because I would've called her on the way home, but I was still phoneless. Thanks to that bitch Charlene, my cell phone got up and walked out of my house. The more I thought about her shysty ass, the more upset I got.

I was now starting to have regrets about dragging Trice into this reality show bullshit. If I would've listened to her from the beginning, I wouldn't be having all of these mixed emotions and she and I would be in a better place. But no, I allowed money to come between us and now I'm kicking myself in the ass for choosing it over my wife.

Hopefully I'll be able to talk to her and we can get to the bottom of what's going on in her head. From this day forward, I'm not letting anyone interfere with my baby. I'd kill somebody behind her if I had to.

I've got to protect me and mines.

26

Charlene

When Leon came back in the house, I thought he was going to jump in my ass about what I told Trice. But he went straight upstairs and acted as if I wasn't even in the house. As much as I didn't want to fuss with him this evening, I was somewhat upset that he wouldn't confront me. I mean, I did tell Trice that I fucked Troy. So why wasn't he grilling me about it? Did he not care? Was he really done with me? Well, whatever was on his mind, it was clear that it wasn't about me and now I knew everything was going downhill from here. Things were going to get worse before they got better.

Once I unpacked my bags, I climbed onto the couch in my TV room so I could wind down. I heard Leon rambling around in our bedroom and then he got quiet all of a sudden. I muted the TV and waited to hear more movement so I could figure out what he was doing up there. But it had gotten so quiet I could've heard a straight pin drop to the floor with no problem. A minute later I heard some mumbling and then it stopped. Then I heard Leon giggle for a few seconds. I knew then he was either on his cell phone or watching TV. Since I hadn't heard any sound come from the TV, I figured he had to be on the phone. Anxiety set in my stomach, so I jumped up from the couch and snuck up the staircase to see if I could find out what was really going on.

When I reached halfway up the staircase, I heard him whisper a few words. They weren't quite clear, but my suspicions were confirmed that he was talking on the phone and he didn't want me to hear his conversation.

I knew I talked a lot of crap and professed that I hated my husband, but this was not the way I wanted this thing to go down. I was tired of being the one with the aching heart, which was why I told Trice I slept with her husband. I got tired of sitting on the sidelines and hearing the rumors about Leon and his fucking tramps. I nearly came close to having a nervous break-down one time, so it felt good not to be on the receiving end this time. I wanted to fuck up his pride and let him see how I felt when I used to catch him cheating. But apparently he wasn't fazed by what I told Trice. The more I thought about it, the motherfucker probably fucked her to get back at me.

Realizing I may have created my own hell storm, my heart began to ache and the knot in my stomach got bigger. I wanted to turn around and head back downstairs, but my heart wouldn't let my body make the turn. I wanted to find out what was going on behind my bedroom door and that's what I did.

When I reached the top of the staircase, I tiptoed to the bedroom quietly, pressed my left ear against the door, and waited patiently for him to utter another word. My heart started beating like crazy and then I heard him laugh.

"Come on now, Trice, you gon' play me like that?" I heard him say.

From the moment I heard her name, that knot I had in my stomach started flipping around uncontrollably. I had also developed a bad taste in my mouth. I mean, why in the world was he talking and laughing with Troy's wife on the fucking phone? Did he fuck her while she laid her stinking ass up in my house? Or did she get played like I did and was only able to suck his dick? Whatever happened, he liked it enough to have her laughing and talking to his grimy ass on the phone.

It took everything within me not to kick down the fucking bedroom door. I also had the urge to douse it with a gallon of gasoline and set it ablaze. I wondered how much longer he'd be smiling and laughing on the phone with Trice then? But then I figured that if I did that, I'd be thrown in jail for a very long time and I would lose my chances of ever getting that money in my hands. I decided that Leon's life wasn't worth the ten thousand, so I remained calm and listened to his conversation a little longer.

What I found while listening to this buster's conversation was huge amounts of ammunition to divorce him. I could bury him and not feel bad about it. He was sealing his fate and he had no idea that I was on the other side of the door, taking it all in.

"Just say the word and I'll be there in a heartbeat," I heard him say. "I told you my marriage with Charlene is over. I'm not even attracted to her anymore. It's been over a month since we last had sex. So that ought to tell you where my head is with that situation," he continued, and then he fell silent.

While I had a chance to soak in everything he'd just said, my mind started running around in circles. I knew there wasn't a chance for us to patch things up, but I had no idea that he wasn't attracted to me anymore. For him to tell her we hadn't had sex in over a month was like a slap in the face. What the fuck was he trying to gain by telling her our business like that? She was the fucking outsider, not me. What the fuck was his problem?

Once again I found myself trying to remain calm so I could finish hearing everything Leon had to say to her. I've been told that when you go snooping around looking for something, you always get more than what you bargain for. So while I continued to eavesdrop on this nigga's conversation, I heard him interrupt her.

"Hey, baby, hold on a minute. Somebody is trying to call me on the other line," I heard him say. "Hello," he said, after he clicked over to the other phone line. And then he fell silent. "Nah, man, she ain't called here," he said, and then he fell silent once again. "Troy, if I knew, man, I would tell you. All she did was hop in the cab, said good-bye, and left," Leon said, and then he fell silent again. "A'ight, I'll let you know if I hear something," he concluded.

After I heard him say hello all over again, I knew he had clicked back over to the other line so he could finish talking to that bitch Trice. At that point, I wanted to bust his motherfucking bubble. I wanted to see his facial expression and let that asshole know that I knew he was on the phone with Trice and I heard his entire conversation with Troy. I didn't know how he would react, but I was willing to see.

But first I wanted to see if he was going to tell her that her husband had just called. From what I heard, it sounded like Trice was somewhere other than with her husband. Because why would he be calling Leon and asking him if he heard from her? Not only that, but also if she wasn't with Troy, then where the hell was she? I knew one thing: Leon knew where she was and as soon as I got the chance, I was going to make sure Troy knew it.

"That was Troy on the other end," I heard him say. "Nah, he's gone now. But he did ask me if I heard from you," Leon continued, and then he paused. "Come on now, how would I look telling him that you're at a hotel?" he whispered. Trice evidently said something and he replied, "Look, I got everything under control on this end. You just handle your end."

I so wished I could get my hands on that bitch's neck. She was fucking up my marriage. Yeah, I lit the fire with my conversation with her and lying on her husband, but what kind of bitch found refuge in another man's arms that damn fast?

I knew she was talking, but I didn't know what she was saying. Then Leon questioned her, "So, when are you going to break the news to him?"

When I heard him ask her that, I knew Leon was referring to her husband. The type of news she planned to break to Troy was beyond me.

Then I figured it had to have something to do with them. If that was the case, then shit was going to get really ugly.

The way Troy felt about Trice, I knew he wouldn't be a happy camper when he found out my husband was keeping information about Trice from him. If he found out they fucked each other during their time together, a storm would brew up in the worst kind of way. And the way I saw it, somebody was going to get it.

While Leon continued to chat with Trice, I began to weigh my options about whether or not to burst into the bedroom. I could either curse him out and go upside his head, or I could act as if I wasn't eavesdropping and kill his ass softly by calling Troy up and telling him everything I knew. Giving Troy the scoop about their little affair would be icing on the cake for me.

I could sit back and watch Leon get his ass kicked and then I could see Trice and Troy's marriage destroyed right before my eyes. Just like me, everybody would feel violated. That would be a win-win situation across the board for me. Raining on Leon's parade was the best revenge I could ever get, since I'd endured all those lonely nights while he stayed out and fucked random bitches. And doubly getting back at Troy for being an asshole when I stayed with him.

Hell yeah! I was going to finally get the payback I deserved. But before I walked away from the bedroom door, I had to find out which hotel she was staying at. I knew when I told Troy she was in a hotel room, he was going to ask me where. So I waited at the door just a little bit longer to see if Leon would slip and mention her whereabouts.

"I'll tell you what. Get some rest and as soon as I take care of my business here, I'll head over there," I heard him tell her, and then he paused. "Whatcha mean?"

I had no idea what the hell he was talking about. Plus I hated the fact that I couldn't hear Trice's responses or conversation. His one-sided conversation truly irritated me.

"Trice, you aren't that far. Remember, it only took me about fifteen to get you from here to Newtown Road. But if I don't get there by the time you get up, just walk next door to Ruby Tuesday and get you something to drink," he told her, and then he said a few more words. It sounded as if he was giving her some type of instructions. A few minutes later, it sounded like he was trying to give her a remedy to get rid of a headache.

I knew one thing: I was getting a headache listening to them. I also felt like I had heard enough information to call Troy so he could tear their whole world apart, and in turn, upset his own world.

I walked away from the bedroom door, raced back downstairs, grabbed my cell phone from the coffee table, and grabbed Troy's cell phone from my purse. I searched for his home number in his contact log and found it underneath the name *Home*. I wasted no time dialing the number. While I waited for him to answer it, I listened for Leon's every movement. I figured since he wanted to be sneaky and talk to Troy's wife behind his back, I was going to do the same fucking thing by talking to Troy.

Finally, on the fourth ring, Troy answered, "Hello," he said.

I cleared my throat. "Troy, this is Charlene."

"What's up?" he asked me. I was surprised he was in a calm mood when he heard my voice. I was expecting some smart-ass comment.

"You just called Leon a few minutes ago, asking about Trice, right?"

"Yeah, why?"

"Because, while you were on one end asking him if he had talked to her since she left our house, she was on the other end," I whispered to avoid Leon from hearing my conversation.

"You bullshitting me!" he roared.

"Nope. I am not bullshitting you. As a matter of fact, he's upstairs in our bedroom talking to her on the phone now. I stood on the other side of the door and heard his entire conversation with her."

"You mean to tell me that nigga is talking to her right now?" he spat, and I could tell that the more he thought about what I had said, the angrier he was becoming.

"Yep. I wanted to blow his cover and kick the fucking bedroom door down, but I figured it wouldn't have done anything but cause us property damage, so I just let him do him. I'm tired of letting him get over on me. So, I decided the only way I'd get him back was to blow up his spot and let you in on what's really going on between him and Trice."

"Charlene, you better not be fucking with me. Because I would really kill a nigga behind my wife!" he snapped.

"I swear I am not lying. He is on the phone with Trice right now. And from what I heard, she didn't leave here in a cab—they got in his car and he dropped her off."

"Please don't tell me that," he begged. He made it painfully clear that the information I was giving him was becoming unbearable.

"I'm sorry, but I don't know what else to say. You want the truth and now I'm giving it to you."

"Leon knows he's a sucker-ass nigga for doing this to me. And I swear, when I see that nigga, I'm gonna rip off his fucking head!"

"I think you ought to wait until we collect our money first," I reasoned.

"You know what? Fuck that money! Your

grimy-ass husband is 'round here plotting with my motherfucking wife and all you can think about is the money?"

"If you know like I do, you'll stop wearing your heart on your sleeve and go for what you know. Now, I'm not saying that money will solve your problems, but I will say that it will put a bandage on it," I replied. It felt good pouring salt on this whole affair between Trice and Leon. And it felt good to hear the pain in Troy's voice. He was taking it very hard while I was dishing the details of Leon's conversation with Troy's wife. That's right. I let the cat out of the bag. And before I'm done with all three of those clowns, they will wish that they never fucked over on me. I will get the last laugh.

"Fuck that! Tell me where that disrespectful-ass nigga took her."

"She's at the SpringHill Marriott Hotel on Newtown Road, trying to figure out what she's going to do about the situation."

"How you know she's at the SpringHill on Newtown Road?"

"Because he told her it would only take him fifteen minutes to get to her and that if he didn't get to her by the time she got up, go next door to the Rudy Tuesday. The only hotel in this area that takes fifteen minutes to reach and has a Ruby Tuesday next door on Newtown Road is the SpringHill Marriott. Now am I right or wrong?" I questioned him, because I had my facts together. He was the one who needed to screw his head on tight. Whether he wanted to believe it or not, his wife was fucking my husband and from the way things looked, they're planning to see each other again.

"Where is Leon now?"

"He's still upstairs in our room."

"Is he still on the phone with her?"

"I think so. Why?"

"Because I want to talk to that nigga. He's got a lot of explaining to do," Troy replied. He sounded like he was grinding his teeth. I couldn't believe how thickheaded this damn man was. Did I really have to tell this lovesick dumb-ass nigga everything to do?

"No. That's not a good idea, 'cause he might deny it. What you need to do is go up to that fucking hotel and wait around and see if he shows up. That way, you'll be able to catch their monkey asses in the act."

Troy paused for a couple of seconds and then said, "Yeah, you're right. I'm gonna go up to the hotel and wait for him to show up."

"Don't kill nobody," I warned him. I was serious when I said that. These types of situations had a way of messing with the mind and confusing the heart. They say there is nothing like a woman scorned, and I agreed with that. But equally as bad or worse was a man whose woman was fucking another dude. Those were the motherfuckers who killed the woman, her lover, and the damn kids, too, if they happened to be around. Plus, I didn't want any blood on my hands.

"It's too late for all that. But I appreciate you calling me with this."

"No problem. My husband needs to be taught a fucking lesson."

"Yeah. And I'm gonna be the one who does it," Troy replied prior to hanging up.

As soon as our call ended, I laid my phone down on the coffee table and smiled. I honestly felt like jumping up and down because it seemed as if I had scored a victory. Troy was on his way up to the hotel where Trice was hiding out. In another hour or so, Leon would be heading that way too. I could see his stupid ass right now smiling on his way to her room like they're going to live happily ever after. Not on my watch. Because when everyone met up, fireworks were going to go off and I was going to be on the sideline laughing my ass off. Yeah, it really felt good to know I was about to see someone else get hurt other than me. When they said misery loved company, they weren't lying.

And the more I thought about it, the more I realized Leon's worthless ass was worth more to me dead than alive. So if Troy killed his monkey ass, I would be sad and hurt—and that was the truth—but those feelings would only last until the insurance check came and cleared.

Right after the check cleared, I was going to pack up my and our son's shit and go on the road to a destination far away. I believed it would serve me some good to start over fresh in another state. With the money from the reality show and the insurance money, I'd be able to do big things for my son and I.

Fuck Leon, Troy, and Trice!

27

Troy

My heart felt like it was dangling from my chest, barely hanging on by a thread. My adrenaline was pumping like I was running a marathon. So as I raced to get to the hotel, all I could think about was how that nigga Leon betrayed me. That motherfucker lied to me and the fact that he's fucking my wife put the nail in the coffin for me.

The way I felt, I could really do some damage to him. When a man loved his woman and found out she cheated on him with another man, that man could literally rip a man's heart from his chest. What was even worse was that the other man was my homeboy, so my pride has been tested and that's not good.

Women were emotional. Men were logical. There was no doubt that women hurt when their men cheated on them. But because of our sense of logic and egotistical ways, cheating hurt us men more. We didn't think it could happen to us. No man believed his woman could or would cheat on him. Even if the relationship was bad, men still possessed that air of dominance that their woman wouldn't do something as stupid as cheating. Knowing that another man slid his dick inside of something we deemed so precious was damaging to our minds. Most men couldn't come back from that. And the way I felt, I didn't think I would be able to do it myself.

Charlene told me Leon said it would take him fifteen minutes to get to the hotel. However, it only took me ten minutes. I didn't remember if I exceeded the speed limit or ran any red lights. All I knew was I had to get there in a hurry and that's what I did.

When I entered the parking lot, I parked my truck on the side of the hotel. My plan was to stay out of sight so Leon wouldn't see me when he got there. But I still had to be in a good position to see all the cars come and go. After I shut off my truck engine, I sat there in complete silence and wondered how I was going to approach this situation. I also wondered how many men had come before me, sitting outside a hotel, motel, restaurant, or house trying to see what was up with his woman or wife. How many men were in this heartbroken fraternity? Who believed in his woman, only to learn she was a liar and the weakest link in the marriage?

Now, I knew I'd done some grimy shit. And I knew I'd fucked a few bitches behind her back. But I'd never let those hoes come between us. Trice was a special person, a diamond in my eyes, and if everything Charlene said was true, I don't think I'd ever look at Trice the same way because my manhood had been challenged. A spear had pierced my heart. Men were logical and we tried to fight our emotions. Emotions made us crazy. That's why men were from Mars. Mars represented the ego and the unknown. A man learning about his woman cheating on him could beat the shit out of the wife and lover or even kill the assholes. And that was what I was battling with. What would I do?

My first thought was to curse her out and maybe smack her ass one good time. But then I figured if I did that, then she would have every right to call the police on my ass and leave me for good. That was my logical side and I was somewhat happy I still possessed some logic in my soul.

So was that what I wanted? I mean, I wanted to get my point across, but I didn't want to go to jail in the process. Damn, what should I do?

That thought was beating me up. Meanwhile, I contemplated how I was going to handle things. My heart spoke to me and convinced me not to wait for Leon because it could and probably would get really ugly. Logic was seeing its way through to my brain, but seeing the both of them together and having an image of the two of them together would probably make me beat the shit out of both of them.

Anyway, I needed to talk to Trice on my own and then I'd be able to draw my conclusion from there. So without giving it any more thought, I took my keys out of the ignition and got out of my truck. I had to see her face. I wanted to know firsthand why she was here and why she felt like she couldn't come home.

I put on a smile when I walked up to the front desk. There was a young black lady waiting for me as I approached the desk. She didn't look a day over twenty-four, so I knew I could manipulate her into giving me Trice's room number.

"Welcome to the SpringHill Marriott," she said.

I looked at her nametag and said, "Hi, Nancy, I'm supposed to meet my wife here, but when I last talked to her, I forgot to get her room number."

"I'm sorry, sir, but I can't give you that information."

"Look, I understand that you have to enforce company policy, but I just talked to her not that long ago and if this would help . . . ," I said, and took my ID card out of my wallet. Three seconds later, I was showing it to her. "Her name is Trice O'Neal. See, we have the same last name."

She took the ID out of my hand and looked at it. And while she looked it over, I chimed in and made her focus on the fact that I had the same last name as her and that if she looked in the system she'd notice that our address was the same.

"Does she have a cell phone?" she asked as she handed me my ID back.

"That's the thing, she told me she was charging it, which was why we were talking on the hotel phone," I lied. I kept a straight face, though. I wanted to come off as honest as I could. "Look, sweetie, I don't want to get you in trouble, so why don't you call my wife's room and ask her if it's okay for you to give me her room number," I continued, and then I gave her the most sympathetic expression I could muster.

She thought to herself for a moment and then she started punching keys on her computer keyboard. A second or two later she looked back at me and said, "Your wife is on the sixth floor in room six-eleven."

I smiled at her and said, "Thank you so much, sweetie."

I almost jumped for joy when the young girl gave me Trice's room number. She had no idea what she had just done.

As I made my way to Trice's room, the palms of my hands started sweating like crazy. So I rubbed them along the sides of my jeans. But by the time I approached her room, my hands felt drenched all over again. I knew that trying to keep them dry was out of the question. When I was involved in some kind of drama, this always happened to me. I knew I had to block it out and continue to do what I came here to do.

I lifted my sweaty hand to knock on the door, but the sound of Trice's voice stopped me. "Leon, why you playing?" she said, and then she giggled.

My heart pounded like crazy and then it sank into the pit of my stomach after I heard her call Leon's name.

"You know I want to, but it's gonna take some time," she continued to talk, and then she paused again. I was wondering what Leon was saying to her. I tried to block out the hurt I was feeling, but I couldn't. I wanted to kick the door in, but I didn't want to bring any attention to myself. The young girl downstairs had already given me the room number when she wasn't supposed to, so I knew I had to be on my best behavior.

"I don't care where we go to eat, just as long as

it's seafood," I heard her say. And from that statement, I knew they were making plans to go out to eat. I couldn't let that happen. So I knocked on her door that instant. "Hold on. Somebody's knocking at the door," I heard her say.

I heard her footsteps as she approached the door. When she pressed her face against the door to look through the peephole, the hole got dark. I knew I startled her by coming there unexpectedly. But this was the only way I was going to be able to get to the bottom of all this madness. Leon was forging a wedge between me and my wife, and I couldn't let that happen. When I saw the light reappear through the peephole, I knew she saw me and had backed away from the door.

"Trice, open the door," I demanded calmly. But she refused to answer me. So I knocked a couple more times. "Trice, baby, please open the door so we can talk." Again she refused to answer me. By now I knew she had told Leon I was at the door, because it had gotten completely silent in the room. The hotel didn't have a balcony, so I figured she'd be in the bathroom trying to figure out what to do. I knocked on the door a few more times.

"Trice, please open the door, baby. We need to talk. I'm not leaving until we do," I told her. I figured I had to let her know that she didn't have any other option but to answer the door because I wasn't going to leave until she did.

Finally, after begging and pleading with her for over five minutes, she opened the door. To see her face was truly a relief. She acted as if she didn't know what to say to me. The fact that she opened the door for me led me to believe that she was willing to hear what I had to say. I smiled at her so she could feel a little more at ease. She held her cell phone pressed tightly against her right ear as she stood in front of the entryway of the room. She made it painfully obvious that she didn't want me coming any farther than where I was, so I didn't press her into letting me come in.

What bothered me was that she acted like she didn't want to end her phone call. I figured Leon told her to keep him on the line so he could hear our entire conversation. But I wasn't trying to have that. She was my fucking wife. Not his. So he needed to get the fuck back before I turned into something they wouldn't want to see.

"I'm listening," she started off, giving me this nonchalant facial expression.

"Are you on the phone with someone?" I asked her, even though I already knew the answer.

She hesitated and then she said, "You said you needed to talk to me. So what is it, Troy?"

I was on the verge of snatching the phone out of her hand so I could have a man-to-man with that nigga, Leon. But I decided against it. I wasn't ready to deal with him yet. I wanted Trice to explain her side before I questioned Leon.

"Can you hang up the phone first?" I asked her as nice as I could.

"No, I can't hang up."

"Who the fuck are you talking to?" I snapped.

She sucked her teeth as if she was more frustrated than me. "Look, Troy, just tell me what you need to talk to me about," she replied.

"Not until you hang up the phone."

"Why is this phone bothering you so much?"

"Because you're my wife and I want to talk to you privately!" I roared, and then I took a couple of steps toward her.

"You didn't think of me as your wife when you were fucking the hell out of Charlene," she spat. I could tell she was really angry because she spit snot out of her mouth with every word she spoke.

I was shocked more than anything. I mean, who could've told her that I fucked Charlene?

"Who the fuck told you that dumb-ass shit? Leon?" I asked. I wanted to know who could have told her that lie. I knew I hadn't fucked Charlene. And Charlene knew I hadn't fucked her, so where did this bullshit come from? I needed to know.

"No, Leon wasn't the one who told me," she answered as she continued to hold her cell phone against her ear.

"Well, who told you, Trice? Because whoever said it lied. I didn't lay a fucking finger on that dirty bitch!" I tried convincing her.

"That ain't what Charlene said," she blurted out.

"Nah, I don't believe that. She couldn't have told you that bullshit."

"Well, she did," Trice assured me as her eyes became glassy. I could see the hurt in her eyes.

"That's not truth. When could she have told you this?" I asked, because I needed answers. At this point, I couldn't care less if that nigga was on the phone. I wanted him to hear every word I had to say, because the way things were looking, that lie about me fucking Charlene had to come from his ass.

"Look, Troy, stop it. I am up to here with your lies," she said as she took a few more steps backward. She grabbed the door handle and acted as if her next step would be to close the door on me. I couldn't have that, so I walked toward her until I was right dead in her face. Without even thinking about it, I immediately snatched her cell from her. She tried her best to get it back from me, but I was stronger and taller than her. I was able to keep her at arm's length with my left arm while I used my right arm to put the phone up to my ear.

She started screaming and jumping up in the air, hoping she could grab her phone back from me. But she didn't have a chance. "Give me my phone back, Troy."

I ignored her and kept her back from me long enough to say what I had to say to this nigga. I had a lot of shit I had to get off my chest. "Leon, this is Troy," I began to say.

"I know who it is," he replied confidently.

"A'ight. Good. Now tell me why the hell is you talking to my motherfucking wife on the phone? What is so important that you gotta talk to my wife? What, y'all fucking now?" I roared.

"That ain't for me to say, homeboy. You gotta ask Trice that question," he told me, and this time he sounded a little cocky.

He gave me the impression he was the mother-fucker and I was some chump-ass nigga from the street. I quickly straightened that out. "Yo, nigga, let me tell you something. I don't know whatcha bitch ass told my wife, but I'ma tell you that you ain't got enough balls to bring that shit over here to me."

"Troy, you think I'm scared of you? Nigga, I will kill you. What, you forgot how I roll?"

"Nigga, do you think I give a damn how you roll? This is my motherfucking wife! I got papers on her. So do yourself a favor and get the fuck off the phone and tend to that greasy-ass bitch you married to."

"I don't give a fuck about no papers. She said she don't want your monkey ass no more. She told me she wanted me. Now you get the fuck off the phone!"

Hearing Leon tell me that Trice told him she didn't want me anymore felt like I had been hit with a ton of bricks. It hurt me to my heart for another man to tell me that my wife didn't want me anymore. I swear, if Leon were in front of me right now, I would kill his motherfucking ass. But since he wasn't there, I had to turn my focus to Trice.

"You told this nigga you didn't want me anymore?"

Trice's eyes became even glassier. As soon as a tear dropped from her right eye, she said, "Yeah, I said it because when I called you the other night, Charlene answered your phone and told me that you were busy taking a shower because you had just finished fucking her."

"Wait, you called and she answered my phone?"

Trice nodded.

I thought for a second and then I said, "That sneaky-ass bitch! She had my phone the whole motherfucking time."

"What are you talking about?" Trice asked me as if she was confused.

I ignored her question and put my focus back on Leon. "Yo, Leon, stay the fuck away from my wife and tell your bitch I said she owes me a phone." After that, I ended the conversation—I pushed the damn END button. I started to smash her phone against the wall, but I didn't want to scare her. I needed to sit down and act as calmly as I could so I could explain what really happened while Charlene was at our house. I couldn't afford to have my wife thinking that I fucked that nasty bitch. So I laid all the cards down on the table.

After I convinced her to take a seat on the bed, I broke everything to her. I even told her the truth about me letting Charlene suck my dick, which was probably why she stole my phone and acted like she hadn't seen it.

"I love you so much, Trice. And if you left me, I wouldn't be able to move on," I told her.

Tears started rolling down her face, one after the other. She kept looking at the door and then she would turn to look back at me. I knew she wanted to tell me something but didn't know how. I figured it had something to do with Leon. And I kind of knew what it was, but I didn't want to hear her say the words. So I put my finger up to her mouth.

"Look, whatever you did doesn't matter. So, just keep it to yourself," I told her. I knew my heart wouldn't have been able to handle her telling me that she fucked Leon. Niggas can't take it when another nigga take their chick's cookie. That shit ain't cool. We become this wounded solider in a war. We can't come back from it.

I tried everything within my power to bring a good vibe back into the room. Trice wasn't crying, but she was still broken up about everything going on. I wished that I could turn back the hands of time, but that was beyond my control. I didn't know how I was going to ever forgive myself for bringing my wife into this bullshit. We were definitely in a fucked-up situation.

She and I tried to watch a movie together, but we couldn't enjoy it. I saw her staring at the wall for long periods of time. The last time I saw my wife like this, it was at a relative's funeral. And knowing this, I knew that she was knee-deep in whatever she was thinking about.

While we were in the room, I offered to order some food, but she declined. I even offered her something to drink, but she declined that as well. I don't like it when another nigga has control over my wife's emotions. That made me look like a chump. And that wasn't what I was. I was a cat who most niggas respected. So, to have this type of shit happen wasn't a good look. I swear it took every ounce of willpower not to hop in my truck and drive all the way to Leon's house and straighten out this whole situation. It didn't matter if he pulled out his pistol or threw up his hands so we could brawl. All I knew was that this shit wasn't going away until it was dealt with. I figured that there was no other way around it.

I needed my wife back. It was as simple as that. She was all I had. And if I had to die to get her back, then so be it. I'd just be a dead motherfucker! But I mean, who knows, that nigga Leon could come up dead himself, especially if he wasn't saying what I needed him to say. Where I'm from, you were either going to get that nigga or he was going to get your ass!

Now you choose and see who comes out on top!

28

Leon

My head was turning with fury. That nigga just invited me to his ass and I was going to take him up on that offer. I knew Troy was a street nigga. But guess what? I was too. I didn't take shit from no one, including his ass. Whether he wanted to believe it or not, his wife wanted me. We made love in my bed more than once. And she told me if things were different, we'd be together. So, having this nigga disrespect me because his woman doesn't want him anymore wasn't a good way to wage war against me. I wasn't about to take this shit lying down. I was going all out on his motherfucking ass. He'd better hope he had come up with an apology by the time I got there. I want that nigga to apologize for the way he talked to me over the phone, and I want him to apologize to Trice for the way he talked to her while I was on the other end listening. If that don't happen, the hotel maids will find a couple of bullet fragments on the floor.

I grabbed my pistol from my sock drawer and headed downstairs. Charlene smiled at me on my way out of the house. I knew the bitch was up to something; I just couldn't put my finger on it. Since I didn't have time to find out what it was, I gave her the middle finger and told her I was leaving her dumb ass and that I'd be back in an hour to pack up all my shit.

"Nigga, I don't give a fuck! Carry your little dick ass!" she spat.

I started to call her a grimy-ass whore, but I refused to waste my energy and my breath. I hated that she was the mother of my son, because she was a lazy, washed-up bitch with bad credit and a bad attitude. I had something better with a lot more class waiting for me to rescue her from her loser husband at the hotel. So I bounced and didn't look back.

I hopped in my car and sped toward Virginia Beach as if my mind were going bad. With my burner in my pocket, I knew I would be all right when I ran up on Troy. I had to admit he had somewhat of an edge on me, because he was bigger and taller. But I knew busting him in the ass with one of these ironclad missiles would bring him down to size. I knew I had to go there and let him know I had fallen in love with Trice and I wasn't going to leave there without her.

When I pulled into the parking lot, I parked my car directly in front of the hotel's revolving doors. Immediately after I turned off the ignition, I jumped out and rushed inside. I heard some lady say good evening, but I ignored her and proceeded toward the elevator. My heart pounded with each step I took. But I blocked it out. I was there to set the record straight with Troy. I was going to tell him the real deal and let him know that Trice was coming home with me. I wasn't concerned about how he would take it. I was only concerned that he knew where I stood with this whole situation. I mean, he can't blame me for stepping on his toes because the nigga fucked my wife first. That left his wife, Trice, out there in the open. She was fair game.

The whole time I was on the elevator, I tried to map out how I was going to approach him. I knew I couldn't walk up on him like I was a punk. I had to hold my head up and let that nigga know that I meant business.

How I was going to hold my gun played a huge part too. I needed to figure out if I was going to have it stick out of my front pocket, hide it underneath my shirt, or hold it in my hand. This was a critical part of my plan to confront him. So, what was a man to do?

By the time I made it off the elevator, I had figured out where my gun was going to be. I realized that it would be better if I stuck it in the waist of my jeans and covered it with my shirt. That way if things didn't get out of hand, I wouldn't have to pull it out.

I knocked on the door as soon as I walked up to it. I thought Troy was going to ask who it was, but he snatched the door open as if he was expecting me. He stood about four inches taller than me and was about fifty pounds heavier. When he spoke, his tone matched his body type.

"You still a hardheaded nigga I see," he said sarcastically.

"Where is Trice?" I asked.

Before he could answer me, she stuck her head out from around the corner of the room. She looked like she had been crying. "You all right?" I asked her.

Before she could answer me, Troy stepped in front of her, blocking my view of her and told me to get lost. But I wasn't having that. "Can you move out of her way so she can answer me?" I asked nicely. I was trying to give that nigga a get-out-of-jail-free card, but he was pressing his fucking luck.

"I ain't going nowhere, nigga. You can take your ass back down to that elevator before shit gets real physical around here."

"Nigga, why don't you make me?" I dared him. I slowly reached for my gun that was tucked away underneath my shirt. And by the time I grabbed a hold to it, Troy rushed toward me.

At that moment I knew I couldn't let him grab a hold of me or I'd be finished. So before he could lay a finger on me, I jumped back a couple steps and then I pulled out my pistol and aimed it at him.

He stopped in his tracks and laughed at me. "Oh, so you pulling out burners on niggas now?" he said. "You know you gon' have to use that, right?" he continued, and then he lunged at me.

Before he got within arm's reach of me, I closed my eyes and pulled back on the trigger. I lost count, but I think I shot the gun two or three times. I knew the power behind these bullets would stop him in his tracks, but I was wrong. And when I realized how wrong I was, Troy was on top of me and I heard Trice in the background screaming her poor little heart out. She screamed for someone to come and help break up Troy and me.

I was lying on my back while he was on top of me. He snuck a couple of blows to my head while I struggled to keep the gun in my hands. I managed to fire two more shots. When I did, I heard a loud thud immediately after. Troy heard it too.

Both of us took our attention off each other and looked inside the room and noticed that Trice was lying on the floor in a pool of her own blood. Troy got off me and rushed to her side.

"Nigga, you shot my motherfucking wife!" he screamed as he tried to lift her up from the floor.

I knew that when I initially came here, I came prepared to disable Troy through any means necessary if he decided that he wanted to run up on me. I had made up my mind that I was going to demolish his ass. But for some strange reason I wasn't living up to my fullest potential. I was shaking like a little bitch. I was even on the verge of having a nervous breakdown. Anxiety sat in the bottom of my stomach and I panicked. I knew at that very moment that I was in a world of trouble. My freedom would be snatched away from me as soon as the police arrived. I wasn't trying to go to jail. I had so much to live for out here on the streets. I mean, if Troy would've let me talk to her, then none of this shit would have happened. It was his fault. Now I had to take the rap for it.

With the gun in my hand, I got up from the floor, somewhat paralyzed. I really didn't know what to do. I knew I didn't want to go to jail, especially since I had had no intention of shooting Trice. I loved her. If Troy had stayed out of my way, then we would all be in a better place right now. But since that didn't happen, shit got a little more complicated, and now I had to come up with another plan.

Without hesitation, I bolted toward the elevator, but before I could reach it, a task force of cops came running toward me.

"Police! Drop your weapon and put your hands up!" a white cop yelled. Behind him were five other cops. They were all dressed in uniform and strategically positioned. My heart dropped. I started to bust a couple shots at them, but then I decided that that would be a dummy move. If I fired off another shot, they'd spray my ass with all the ammunition they had, so I decided to drop my gun and give up. This was the only way I knew that would secure my life.

"Get down on the floor!" the same cop yelled.

I looked at Trice one last time. I saw her losing consciousness, but Troy kept talking to her, hoping he could keep her alive. She looked so pitiful and I didn't want her to die. She didn't deserve it. All she wanted was for a man to love her. And I wanted to be that man. But Troy wasn't trying to let me take his place without a fight. Unfortunately, Trice got caught in the crossfire.

"I said drop your weapon and get down on

the floor!" the cop yelled once more. Not even a second later I threw my pistol down on the floor and then I got down on my knees and assumed the position. Two cops rushed me while one of the other cops picked my gun up from the floor.

While I was being handcuffed, I heard Troy pleading with the cops to get a paramedic to Trice before he lost her. "Sir, they just arrived in the lobby of the hotel, so they'll be up in a few minutes," one cop explained.

"He's gonna have to move out of the way when they do get up here," I heard another cop say.

By this time I couldn't see what was going on. I heard Troy talking to Trice in an effort to keep her conscious. "Just hold on, baby. It's gonna be all right. The paramedics are on their way up here right now." She didn't respond, but I was sure that she heard him.

A few minutes after the cop lifted me up from the floor in handcuffs, the paramedics stepped off the elevator. It was a black male and a white female. "The paramedics are on the floor. Clear the way," I heard another cop announce. The cop who had me standing right by his side pushed me to the side. I mean this cat literally shoved me into the wall. I didn't make a fuss about it because all the attention needed to be on Trice. Her life hung in the balance, and if I had to get roughed up just so the paramedics could pass me to get to Trice, then so be it. It was about her. Not me.

"Sir, you're gonna have to move to the side and let the paramedic do their job," I heard another say.

"Is she gonna be okay?" Troy asked. His voice sounded weak. It almost sounded like he was about to cry.

"Sir, we're going to do everything within our power," a female paramedic assured him.

"Please do. I don't know what I'll do if my wife dies." Troy began to cry.

"Just stay back, sir, and I assure you that we're gonna do all that we can."

"What is your full name, sir?" the cop who handcuffed me asked.

"Leon Bunch," I said.

"Do you have any more weapons of any kind on your person?"

"No, sir."

"You do know that you will be charged with attempted murder?"

"Yes, sir, I'm aware of that."

"Well, I'm gonna have my partner read you your rights. And once that's done, we're gonna take you down to the precinct so we can process you. Now, do you have any questions?"

"No, sir, I don't," I said. I mean, what did he

want me to say? I was caught red-handed. I had the gun in my hand and the person I shot was lying on the floor in her own pool of blood.

I'd be lucky if I didn't get a life sentence once this was over. What would be even worse was if Trice died, I'd be faced with a murder rap. Boy, I would be fucked. And what was a slap in the face was that I'd end up with nothing.

Aside from my son, I had nothing else to live for. I hated my wife. She was a thorn in my side and I wanted her gone out of my life for good. If I could get someone to kill her, I'd do it. Seeing her body lying in a coffin would bring me so much joy. I'd be drama-free. In addition to that, I would not have to hear her mouth. She would be a distant memory. What a joy that would be to me.

Five minutes into all the chaos around me, the paramedic finally got Trice stable. And as they rolled her out of the hotel on the stretcher, I got a quick look at her. She had her eyes closed when they wheeled her by me, but I was still able to get a look at her. They had an oxygen mask covering her nose and mouth, so I knew there was a chance they might be able to save her. I just hoped and prayed that she'd be all right. I wouldn't be able to live with myself if she didn't. I guess we would find out soon enough.

29

Charlene

I was restless and curious about what was happening at the hotel. I borrowed the car of a friend, who lived on the next street over, and made my way to the hotel. I was surprised when I saw the police cars and the ambulance parked out front.

The ambulance meant someone was hurt. And seeing police was a tell-tale sign that someone was going to jail. I had no idea who it could've been, but I was sure going to find out.

I felt indifferent to the whole situation. I didn't want anyone dead. If anyone had to die, I hoped it was Leon so I could get the insurance money. And in the process, I hoped this love triangle ruined Troy and Trice's marriage—they didn't deserve to be happy. Both of them were phony as hell.

As I walked closer to the crowd, I saw my dumb-ass husband, Leon, sitting in the back of the police car in handcuffs looking pitiful and miserable as hell. *What the fuck?* I shook my head. Dumb, stupid fuck.

Seconds later, the paramedics rushed a stretcher out of the hotel with Trice lying on it. She wore an oxygen mask on her mouth and she had other stuff like an IV hooked up to her. Troy walked alongside Trice as the paramedic pushed the stretcher toward the ambulance. Once they approached the ambulance, Troy climbed in the back of it immediately after the paramedics locked in Trice's stretcher. Right after the door to the ambulance was closed, the vehicle drove away. While I stood there, I realized how serious this situation had gotten. I had no idea why Trice was taken away in an ambulance until I heard a couple of hotel guests whispering a few feet away from me. There was a white, older couple standing near the sliding door of the front entrance of the hotel. Standing next to them were two Hispanic housekeepers and a black gentleman, who looked like he was also a hotel guest, toting a duffel bag. I walked causally over to the two housekeepers and the black guy and inquired about what had happened. The black guy spoke up first. "The ladies just told me that the lady that left in the ambulance was shot by the guy that's sitting in the back of the police car."

I turned around and took another look at Leon. He tried to hold his head down, but I saw his silly-looking face. I knew he felt like a fucking fool, coming all the way here to confront a man about another woman when he had his own wife. I just felt discontent in my heart for this dumb bastard. I mean, who does that? There was no way I'd ever run up on a bitch behind her husband. That shit didn't make sense to me. Leon was a loser and I had to accept it.

"Where did he shoot her?" I asked him.

Before the guy answered my next question, the two housekeepers walked away. I assumed they had to go back to work. So I gave him my full attention. "I'm not sure."

"Those two housekeepers didn't tell you?"

"Those two housekeepers were Mexican, and they don't speak a lot of English, but I did understand them when they said the two guys were fighting and while they were fighting the lady got shot."

"Where did it happen?"

"They said in the hotel room."

"Well, I know they've got the entire hotel floor blocked off to keep anybody from going up there."

"I'm sure they do. But I just got here. And I

was about to go inside to check in, but I don't think that's going to be a good idea," he said.

"I don't blame you." I commented. And then I turned my focus back to my dumb-ass husband. I noticed that he had lifted his head, but he wasn't looking in my direction; he was looking at three cops who were standing in a huddle talking to one another. I sure wished that I were a fly swooping around in that circle because inquiring minds want to know what really went on before the tragedy happened.

The black guy finally left me standing by the sliding glass alone. He got back into his car and left the scene. I couldn't blame him. Too much drama if you asked me. And to know that Trice left here with a gunshot wound wasn't what I had expected. I knew Leon wanted to make a statement and show Troy he wasn't a wimp. But this shooting situation meant that he took this shit to another level. He's going to do a ton of prison time for another man's pussy. Now how stupid does that sound? That nigga hasn't ever defended my honor and I was his wife. He used to stare a nigga down if he caught him looking at my ass. But that was it.

The more I thought about how that dumb-ass nigga treated me, the more I got disgusted with his ass. He had become this liability in my eyes. There was nothing he'd be able to do for our son or myself considering he was on his way to jail. So, I knew it was time for me to put a plan into motion.

Five minutes had passed and Leon finally looked up and saw me. His facial expressions told me a lot. I could tell immediately how bummed he was from the mess he made. I thought he'd try to say a few words so I could read his lips, but he didn't move his lips. Instead of clowning him or giving him the finger like he did me earlier, I let well enough alone. I knew he'd call me from jail once they processed him in and gave him his first phone call. And if I'm wrong and he doesn't try to reach out to me, then it was his loss.

When I had seen enough, I headed back to the car that I'd driven to the scene. And before I pulled away, I pulled up to the police car as close as I could and shook my head back and forth to let him know how stupid he looked. He just sat there with the dumbest expression he could muster. Then he put his head back down. I wasn't too happy after he put his head back down. I wanted him to look me dead in the face so he could see me getting the pleasure of seeing him handcuffed in the back of that police car. I wanted him to see that I finally had the last laugh and that I had the upper hand. He had already ruined his fucking life fucking with Troy's wife, but I had the nail to seal his coffin. Unfortunately for him, that was what I planned to do.

I had had enough of staring at this fucking loser, so I drove back toward my house in Norfolk. During the drive, I began to think about how I was going to get the entire ten thousand dollars. With Leon in jail, I was in control of the money the network execs promised us. Ten thousand dollars would do me a lot of good. All I'd need for Leon to do was sign the back of the check and hand it back to me. I'd take care of the rest. Me and my son were going to live large out here in these streets. Me and my son were going to be hood rich. And who knew, I may just be able to find myself a new man and a new daddy for my son. It wouldn't be hard to do. Niggas come a dime a dozen these days. And the fact that I was going to inherit a pocketful of cash, I was going to be all right.

You can mark my words on that.

30

Troy

The paramedics sped down the emergency room corridor with Trice. I was only a few steps behind them. They delivered her to three different nurses and one of the ER physicians that were on call. I was stopped in my tracks when the hospital staff whisked Trice off into the operating room for emergency surgery. "I'm sorry, sir, but this is as far as you go," the nurse told me.

"Is she going to be all right?" I sobbed. I was falling apart on the inside. My whole world seemed like it was going to fall apart.

"Sir, I need to know what relation that woman is to you," she continued.

"She's my wife." I continued to sob uncontrollably. My heart was beating erratically. My mind was racing and I couldn't make sense of anything. Everything around me started looking like a great big blur.

"Is she allergic to anything?" she wanted to know.

"No. She's not," I managed to say.

"Well, I'm gonna need you to go to admin and start her paperwork," she instructed me as she pointed me into the right direction.

"When will I know if everything is okay with her?" I asked. I needed to know when I could expect to hear something. My wife was all I had. She was my lifeline, and if she died on me today, my life would be over too.

"I can't say right now. But someone will come and talk to you as soon as we know something," she assured me.

"Okay," I said. I searched her face, hoping she'd give me a little more hope than I had. But she didn't. She left me standing there and went back to where the medical staff was operating on Trice.

At that moment, I somehow made my way to the emergency room intake worker. I took a seat on the chair in front of the glass window and told the white woman sitting on the other side of the glass that I was there to fill out paperwork for my wife.

"What's your wife's name?" she asked me.

"Trice O'Neal. The paramedics just brought her in. She was shot," I began to explain.

"Do you have her ID card?"

"No. We left her purse at the hotel."

"Does she have health insurance?"

"Yes, she's on my insurance."

"Can I see your driver's license and y'all insurance card?" she asked.

I handed her my driver's license and the health insurance card after I took it out of my wallet. She took them both and placed them on the desk in front of her. She went on to ask me a few questions about Trice. And after I answered all her questions, I signed a few forms. When I was done, I was told to go into the waiting room and stay there until someone came for me.

I got up from the chair and headed into the waiting room. It was packed wall to wall with people seeking medical attention. But I knew that no one sitting among me had a loved one fighting for their life. My heart was aching severely. I couldn't think straight. My mind kept replaying the entire incident in my head. I mean, how dare that motherfucker come and try to check me behind my wife? He was wrong for stepping to me about a woman that belonged to me. I had papers on her ass. Not him! So, to have him come there with his pistol like he intended to shoot me was some fucked-up shit. That nigga was bold as hell. I swear I couldn't wait to see him again. He'd better hope that I never see his stupid ass on the streets because if I do, I'm going to rip his fucking heart out of his chest. That's my word!

An hour passed and I still hadn't heard anything from the doctors who were operating on Trice. I became so impatient that I got up from my chair and went into the emergency room without being seen. I walked slowly through the doctors' and nurses' quarters like I knew where I was going. A couple of the nurses and LPNs smiled at me as I passed them. I was surprised that neither of them asked me why I was back there, but I guess God was on my side. He knew I needed to see about Trice.

I stayed on course and made my way back to the operating room I remembered they took Trice into. It was down a long corridor and it seemed like everyone coming from that direction was wearing a white doctor's coat. I panicked immediately because I didn't have a fucking lab coat. How would I be able to see my wife? At that point I figured it was do or die. I had already snuck back here; I couldn't turn back now. And without a moment's notice, I started speed walking as fast as I could. I shot by one nurse and an X-ray tech. Both were women and the nurse tried to stop me. "Excuse me, sir, where are you going?" she asked.

I didn't answer her. I kept bolting back toward

the operating room where Trice was. I refused to wait any longer for someone to come and tell me how my wife was doing. No way. I was going to find out on my own.

"I'm sorry, sir, but you can't go back there," the nurse yelled.

"She's right, sir. No one is permitted back there," the X-ray tech yelled.

I continued to ignore them both, and they started walking behind me. I knew they were going to try to stop me, so I took off running. "We've got a runner!" I heard someone yell.

"I just want to see if my wife is all right," I yelled so everyone would understand why I was back here.

A few feet behind me I heard footsteps on my trail, but I couldn't worry about that. My mission was to see my wife. That was it. I counted the distance in front of me. I only had a thirty-foot stretch. It was now or never.

"Get him! He's headed for the operating room," I heard a woman yell.

I looked back and saw four men and the two women running in my direction. I couldn't let them catch me. I turned back around and pulled everything within me to press forward.

I ran as fast as I could. And I finally made it to the operating room Trice was in. I lifted my head and peered through the glass in the door and my heart sank into the pit of my stomach. I pushed both doors open. "What are you doing? Take that sheet off of her. She's not dead!" I screamed in agony.

The doctor was pulling off his gloves when he looked up. "Somebody get him out of here!" he yelled. And immediately I was tackled to the floor. The medical staff from every inch of this hospital grabbed some part of my body to restrain me. I tried to fight them back, but I couldn't. My body felt too weak. Seeing the lifeless body covered up with a sheet on the operating table took a lot out of me. I gave up. It was over for me.

I can't go on with my life.

31

Leon

"Put him in holding cell three," the correctional officer instructed the cop who arrested me.

The jail cell was dark, filthy, and smelled of urine. I gagged at least fifty times in the first ten minutes. There was another cat lying down on the only bench in the cell. He was a younger black dude. He had to be in his early twenties. While he lay on his back with his arm covering his eyes, I stood by the bars so I could see what was going on around me.

For some reason the cop who brought me in disappeared. I watched as one correctional officer processed a white chick while another correctional officer acted like they were typing something into the computer. These mother-fuckers looked like they were dragging their feet. I knew then that I was going to be in this cell for a very long time. I knew I wouldn't be able to stand on my feet for a long time, so I took a seat on the floor near the wall. I sat there for at least fifteen minutes before the homeboy lying on the bench looked up and sparked a conversation with me. "I was gon' see how long you was gon' stand there before your feet got tired. Them crackers gon' have you waiting in here all day long," he said.

"Man, I ain't worried about that. I've got bigger fish to fry," I told him. It didn't matter how long I was going to be in this cell. My main concern was on whether or not the magistrate was going to give me a bond. I needed to get out of this place so I could see if Trice was going to be all right.

"Whatcha in here for?" he asked me. "What they charge you with?"

"Attempted murder."

"Damn, nigga, who you shoot?"

"It's a long story," I replied, and then I placed my face in my hands.

"You better hope they don't put you in front of that black lady magistrate because that bitch is crazy. And she ain't gon' give you shit. She denies everybody bonds."

"Did they take you in front of her?"

"Yeah and I ain't get shit. And what's so fucked up is that I only came in here for child support."

"Oh yeah, if she didn't give you a bond, I know she ain't gonna give me one," I said. I wasn't too happy about the idea that I may not be able to get out of here. In addition to seeing how Trice was, I needed to get that ten-thousand-dollar check before Charlene got her hands on it. I had things that I needed done and I knew she wouldn't take care of them. The way she looked at me from the car that belonged to our neighbor, I knew she was done with me. She didn't know it, but I watched her from the corner of my eye. I saw her when she shook her head at me. I knew she was disgusted with me. And I knew she wanted to rub this whole incident in my face, but my pride wouldn't let me give her the satisfaction. She would go to the lengths of spitting at me if she could. She would've punched me in the face if she had been within arm's reach. Charlene was one grimy bitch. And she wasn't a chick any nigga would want to fuck with because she had some sneaky ways.

A couple hours passed and I was finally put in front of a magistrate. It wasn't the black chick the guy in the cell talked about. I sat down in front of a white dude. I found out that it really didn't matter which magistrate I saw, because this dude dealt me a bad hand too. He denied my bail, so I had to sit my ass in jail until I saw a judge. I guess I was in for a long ride. I couldn't say who'd ride with me. But if I wanted to get Charlene on board, I was going to have to do some heavy convincing that I was sorry about everything that happened and that I truly loved her. I knew I would also have to convince her that I'd never betray her again. Chicks loved it when a nigga poured his heart out. I would have to be sincere too. If I wasn't, I was going to be up shit creek.

The correctional officer who processed me in the system and handed me an orange jumpsuit allowed me to make a phone call. I fought with the decision whether I should call my parents or Charlene. I knew that if I called her, she may not have answered my call. And if I called my parents, they'd be really disappointed. My mother especially because she had heart trouble. She'd be devastated and I'd never forgive myself if I was the cause of her getting sick or having a heartache. She meant the world to me, which was why I decided to call Charlene instead.

I dialed our home phone number and crossed my fingers that she'd answer it. And to my surprise, she did. She even accepted my phone call. I couldn't fucking believe it. "What do you want?" she snarled into the phone.

I knew she was upset with me for what had happened, so I gave her all the room she needed to vent. I deserved it. "Thanks for answering my call," I said as politely as I could. I was at this girl's mercy. And if I didn't want her to hang up on me, I had to say the right things.

"Don't give me that bullshit, Leon! What the fuck do you want?" she screamed. She knew I was playing games with her and she wasn't feeling it either.

"What bullshit, Charlene? I just called to tell you that the magistrate denied my bail and that I wasn't coming home anytime soon, in case our son called and asked to speak with me," I explained. I tried to be as calm as I possibly could.

"Do you think I give a fuck about you getting out of jail?" she continued to scream.

"Look, I know you're mad with me because of what happened. But you need to let me give you my side of the story."

"I don't care to hear your side of the story. You told me that you were leaving me when you left this house. And then you carry your dumb ass over to the hotel where Trice and Troy were and started shooting shit up like you were a fucking vigilante or something. That was some bold shit you did. I'm almost close to believing that you were on some bath salts or something."

"Nah, I wasn't on no bath salts."

"Well, you should've been because anyone with a sane mind who goes around and starts busting his fucking gun behind another man's wife is stupid. I mean, do you know how I'm going to look when everyone finds out about this?"

"I know, Charlene. I fucked up."

"You sure did. And guess what?"

"What?" he said calmly.

"I'm leaving your dumb ass in jail to rot! I'm taking our son and we're moving out of this house. So kiss my ass!" she screamed, and then she disconnected our call.

I knew my marriage was over before I dialed the number. And what's more devastating than anything was that I lost Trice in the process too.

I guess I fucked up royally this time.

Sneak Peek
Wife Extraordinaire Returns
In stores September 2014

Charlene

My weave was sweated completely out and the hair of my Chinese bang was plastered to my forehead by the time I arrived at the prison. I had been running, rushing, and killing myself to get there since I changed my mind about visiting Leon at the last minute. I had just made the last visitor cutoff time. I was usually there for the first visit time.

I shifted my weight from one foot to the next while I waited in the processing line. My feet were killing me and my legs were cold. I had on the things Leon always required me to wear—my come-fuck-me pumps and the shortest miniskirt in my closet, so he could finger my pussy under that table when the COs weren't looking.

"Next!" I heard the processing CO scream out. I moved to the counter and extended my ID to her.

"Leon Bunch," I said. I watched as her fingers pecked the computer keyboard rapidly.

"Who you say again?" the CO asked me, her face crinkled into a frown.

"Leon Bunch," I repeated, furrowing my eyebrows at her as if she was a stupid ass. She started pecking again and then she looked at me strangely.

"Miss, I'm sorry, but Mr. Bunch already had a visit today," the CO informed me. My heart started pumping fast as hell and more sweat broke out on my head.

"That's impossible! I'm the only person that visits him and I just got here," I told her with much attitude. "Check your little system again. You must have the wrong Leon Bunch!" I snapped. I was looking at the bitch like she had ten heads and was a fire-breathing dragon. The CO pecked on some more buttons; then she chuckled like I had made a fucking joke. I was gritting on her like I wanted to smack the hell out of her.

"Sorry to inform you that we only have one Leon Bunch in our system. You can look for yourself and check the date of birth while you're at it. Here is his visitor log for this week," the CO replied smugly as she turned the computer monitor so I could see it. She used her index finger to point to the line where Leon's visits were listed. I moved in for a closer look. When I read Leon's Tuesday and Saturday visitor log, my legs got weak and my knees almost buckled. I was blinking rapidly to keep the tears from falling out of my eyes and to try to save face in front of the CO.

"See, a Trice O'Neal visited both days, so you can't be the *only* one visiting him," the CO said, putting the emphasis on the word *only* I had used earlier. I let out a nervous little chuckle and placed my hand over my chest like I was relieved.

"Oh, that's just his sister. I thought I would have to get crazy," I laughed, trying to play it off. The room was actually spinning around and I felt an overwhelming urge to vomit. I didn't know what to do next. Here I was neglecting my son's baseball game, giving up my morning, rushing to the prison, and all along this motherfucker was still seeing that bitch Trice.

"That's what they all say when they find out," the CO said sarcastically, with a look on her face that made me want to just punch the shit out of her.

"So you have to either wait until Tuesday or next Saturday," the CO followed up. "I'm going to have to ask you to move aside so I can process this line of people," she instructed me.

"Can I get a printout of that screen?" I asked

her. She looked at me as if I was crazy at first, and then she looked around. She used her computer mouse to click something. Then she slid the paper to me.

"I'm not supposed to do this, but I'm a woman too. I know how it feels to be lied to when you bust your ass to be there for these niggas while they are locked up," the CO whispered. I couldn't say anything to her, because she was absolutely right. I was just happy she believed in sisterhood.

"Next!" the CO called out, giving me the eye to move along.

I stumbled to the left. I felt as if my world was off kilter. My insides were boiling and I didn't know if I was more mad or hurt. I got back on the shuttle bus that took visitors to the main gate and parking lot. I rushed to my car and once I was inside, I broke down crying. I kept reading the paper over and over again. Seeing that bitch's name made me crazy. I slammed my hands on my steering wheel so hard that the skin on my knuckles busted. If it were Trice's face, she would've been beaten bloody.

"You motherfucker! I'm out here struggling and busting my ass. Letting men feel up my pussy and squeeze my breasts for you and this is the thanks I get? I hate you, Leon! I fucking hate you, you son of a bitch!" I screamed at the top of my lungs as if Leon could somehow telepathically hear me.

I was so enraged that I didn't even realize I had also broken four of my newly done nails and my fingertips were bleeding too. My heart hadn't ached this badly since the first time I learned this lying, cheating-ass nigga was fucking another bitch on the side.

We had been together for a year and I was six months pregnant with our son when this young chick from around my way came to my house to confront me about her relationship with Leon. She had knocked on my door and when I answered, she immediately sucker punched me in the face and caught me off guard. My nose had gushed blood and by the time Leon had gotten to the door, the girl's friends had pulled her back down the steps.

While I tried to get the bleeding under control with paper towels, I could hear the girl outside of my house yelling about how she had been fucking Leon for the past six months and that every time I kissed Leon, I was tasting her pussy. Then she said she knew I was having a baby boy, because Leon had told her I went to my sonogram appointment alone since he didn't believe the baby was his. The girl also knew my due date and told me where I had been the night before.

I was floored. But that's how I knew the girl wasn't lying about fucking with Leon. How else would she know Leon had ditched me and made me go to the sonogram appointment alone? How else would she have known I was with my girl-friends the night before and my due date?

That bitch knew so much information she could tell me my last fucking meal. Leon was a lame ass for telling her my damn business. I was devastated and embarrassed because the whole entire neighborhood was outside watching the scene. Leon couldn't say shit but *sorry*. He knew he was cold busted, red-handed. Of course, he got me to stay. To this day, I don't know why I did.

I knew Leon and I hadn't met under the greatest of circumstances. I had been fucking one of his other friends when I started messing with Leon behind his friend's back. Although that was foul, I had never disrespected Leon in public or by having any cats I fucked with con-front him. My past before him was something he had to deal with. If he didn't want me, a girl who had fucked half of Norfolk, then he shouldn't have made me wifey.

After the first cheating incident with Leon, it was like the flood gates opened with him and other chicks. Leon was the disrespectful type of cheater. As foul as it sounded, I wished he would have kept his shit on the low, out of sight, out of mind. No, not his trifling ass. He had bitches calling my house and coming over to curse me out. He would stay out nights with no explanation and come home smelling like stale pussy and perfume.

And my stupid ass put up with all that bullshit. I stayed through it all, but I completely checked out of our relationship. I stopped cooking for him, washing his clothes, or working to help him pay bills. I felt like, *if you want to be a fucking dog, then you take care of yourself.*

Of course, Leon used that shit against me. When we did the spouse trade, Troy told me that Leon used to call me lazy and that I refused to help him pay bills. Leon painted the picture that I just sat around eating all day doing nothing. Hearing that shit hurt me, but of course, I played tough like it didn't. Leon liked to tell one side of the story, but he never told on himself. He never told the reason I stopped doing shit for him was because he was a low-down dirty dog.

But the most fucked up time of all was now. Of all of the times he had cheated, this was the fucking worst I'd ever felt.

He was locked the fuck up and still being a motherfucking dog. And no less with this bitch Trice! No, this wouldn't be the last time Leon would hear from me. I was going to make sure of that.

I finally pulled myself together. After thinking back on shit and all the things Leon put me through, I roughly wiped the tears from my face and I went from hurt to full-out mad as hell. I inhaled a deep breath and started my car. I had someplace important to go before I went home. I was already calculating my plan for revenge in my head. My mind raced a mile a minute too.

I kept picturing Trice's face in my mind. Then I would see Leon's. Those images just fueled the fire raging inside of me.

"You want to fuck with me, Leon! You wait and see what I have in store for your mother-fucking ass!" I gritted through clenched teeth as I pulled away from the prison.

"And, Trice, you bitch, you just wait. You think you skated death once, well, you won't skate a second time, bitch! I fucking promise you that shit," I hissed as I clutched the steering wheel so tight my busted knuckles burned.

It was going to be on and popping now. I was driving like a bat out of hell to my destination. My insides churned with anticipation of what was to come. I had a whole new fucking mission in mind. Trice and Leon had fucked over the wrong bitch!

The saying goes that there is nothing worse

than a woman scorned! Well, I was about to show Leon and Trice that there was nothing worse than fucking over Charlene!

They wanted a fight, well, Charlene is declaring a motherfucking war! Believe that!

From *Fistful of Benjamins*
"Special Delivery" by Kiki Swinson
Available October 2014 wherever books and
ebooks are sold.

Prologue

"**O**h my God, Eduardo. What do you think they will do to us? I don't want to die. . . . I can't leave my son," I cried, barely able to get my words out between sobbing and the fact that my teeth were chattering so badly.

The warehouse type of room we were being held captive in was freezing. I mean freezing like we were sitting inside of a meat locker type of freezing. I could even see puffs of frosty air with each breath that I took. I knew it was summertime outside, so the conditions inside where we were being held told me we were purposely being made to freeze. The smell of sawdust and industrial chemicals were also so strong that the combination was making my stomach churn. Eduardo flexed his back against mine and turned his head as much as the ropes that bound us together allowed. He was trembling from the sub-zero conditions as well.

"Gabby, just keep your mouth shut. If we gon' die right now, at least we are together. I know I ain't say it a lot, but I love you. I love you for everything you did and put up with from me. I am sorry I ever let you get into this bullshit from the jump. It wasn't no place for you from day one, baby girl," Eduardo whispered calmly through his battered lips. With everything that had happened, I didn't know how he was staying so calm. It was like he had no emotion behind what was happening or like he had already resigned himself to the fact that we were dead. In my opinion, his ass should've been crying, fighting, and yelling for the scary men to let me go. Something. Eduardo was the drug dealer, not me, so maybe he had prepared himself to die many times. I hadn't ever prepared myself to die or to be tied up like an animal, beaten, and made to wait to possibly get my head blown off. This was not how I saw my life ending up. All I had ever wanted was a good man, a happy family, a nice place to live, and just a good life.

"I don't care about being together when we die, Eduardo! You forget I have a son? Who is going to take care of him if I'm dead over something I didn't do?" I replied sharply. A pain shot through my skull like someone had shot me in the head. I was ready to lose it. My shoulders began quaking as I broke down in another round of sobs. I couldn't even feel the pain that had previously permeated my body from the beating I had taken. I was numb in comparison to the pain I was feeling in my heart behind leaving my son. I kept thinking about my son and my mother, who were probably both sitting in a strange place wondering how I had let this happen to them. That was the hard part, knowing that they were going to be innocent casualties of my stupid fucking actions. I should've stuck to carrying mail instead of stepping into the shit that had me in this predicament. I was the dummy in this situation. I was so busy looking for love in all the wrong places. I had done all of this to myself.

"Shhh. Don't cry. We just have to pray that Luca will have mercy on us. I will try to make him believe that it wasn't us. I'll tell him we didn't do it. We weren't responsible for everything that happened," Eduardo whispered to me.

"But he's the one who got us out so fast. I keep thinking that he only did that because he thought we might start talking. He got us out just so he could kill us. Don't you see that? We are finished. Done. Dead," I said harshly. The tears were still coming. It was like Eduardo couldn't get what I was saying. We were both facing death and I wasn't ready to die!

"You don't know everything. Maybe it was

something else. Let me handle—" Eduardo started to tell me, but his words were clipped short when we both heard the sound of footsteps moving toward us. The footsteps sounded off like gunshots against the icy cold concrete floors. My heart felt like it would explode through the bones in my chest and suddenly it felt like my bladder was filled to capacity. The footsteps stopped. I think I stopped breathing too. Suddenly, I wasn't cold anymore. Maybe it was the adrenaline coursing fiercely through my veins, but suddenly I was burning up hot.

"Eduardo Santos," a man's voice boomed. "Look at you now. All caught up in your own web." The man had a thick accent, the kind my older uncles from Puerto Rico had when they tried really hard to speak English.

"Luca . . . I . . . I . . . can . . . ," Eduardo stuttered, his body trembling so hard it was making mine move. Now I could sense fear and anguish in Eduardo's voice. That was the first time Eduardo had sounded like he understood the seriousness of our situation.

"Shut up!" the man screamed. "You are a rat, and in Mexico rats are killed and burned so that the dirty spirit does not corrupt anything around it," the man called Luca screamed. I squeezed my eyes shut, but I couldn't keep the tears from bursting from the sides.

I was too afraid to even look at him. I kept my head down, but I had seen there were at least four more pairs of feet standing around. Eduardo and I had been working for this man and had never met him. I knew he was some big drug kingpin inside the Calixte Mexican drug cartel that operated out of Miami, but when I was making the money, I never thought of meeting him, especially not under these circumstances. I was helping this bastard get rich and couldn't even pick him out of a police lineup if my life depended on it.

"Please, Luca. I'm telling you I wasn't the rat. Maybe it was Lance. . . . I mean, I just worked for him. He was the one responsible to you. He was the one that kept increasing everything. I did everything I could to keep this from happening," Eduardo pleaded his case, his words rushing out of his mouth.

"Oh, now you blame another man? Another cowardly move. Eduardo, I have people inside of the DEA who work for me. I know everything. If I didn't pay off the judge to set bail so I could get you and your little girlfriend out of there, you were prepared to sign a deal. You were prepared to tell everything. Like the fucking cocksucking rat that you are. You know nothing about death before dishonor. You would've sold out your own mother to get out of there. You failed the fucking test, you piece of shit," Luca spat, sucking his teeth. "Get him up," Luca said calmly, apparently unmoved by Eduardo's pleas.

"Luca! Luca! Give me another chance, please!" Eduardo begged, his voice coming out as a shrill scream. His words exploded like bombs in my ears. Another chance? Did that mean that Eduardo had snitched? Did that mean he put me in danger when I was only doing everything he ever told me to do? Did Eduardo sign my death sentence without even telling me what the fuck he was going to do? I immediately thought about my family again. These people obviously knew where I lived and where they could find my mother and my son. A wave of cramps trampled through my guts. Before I could control it, vomit spewed from my lips like lava from a volcano.

"What did you do to me, Eduardo?" I coughed and screamed through tears and vomit. I couldn't help it. I didn't care anymore. They were going to kill me anyway, right? "You fucking snitch! What did you do?" I gurgled. I had exercised more loyalty than Eduardo had. The men who were there to kill us said nothing and neither did Eduardo. I felt like someone had kicked me in the chest and the head right then. My heart was broken.

Two of Luca's goons cut the ropes that had kept Eduardo and I bound together. It was like they had cut the strings to my heart too. Eduardo didn't even look at me as they dragged him away screaming. I fell over onto my side, too weak to sit up on my own. Eduardo had betrayed me in the worst way. I was just a pawn in a much, much bigger game. And all for what? A few extra dollars a week that I didn't have anything to show for now except maybe some expensive pocketbooks, a few watches, some shoes, and an apartment I was surely going to never see again. Yes, I had been living ghetto fabulous, shopping for expensive things that I could've never imagined in my wildest dreams, but I had lost every dollar that I had ever stashed away for my son as "just in case" money. I had done all of this for him and in the end I had left him nothing.

"Please. Please don't kill me," I begged through a waterfall of tears as I curled into a fetal position. With renewed spirit to see my son, I begged and pleaded for my life. I told them I wasn't a snitch and that I had no idea what Eduardo had done. I got nothing in response. There was a lot of Spanish being spoken, but I could only understand a fraction of it; so much for listening to my mother when she tried speaking Spanish to me all of my life.

"I promise I didn't speak to any DEA agents or the police. Please tell Luca that it wasn't me," I cried some more, pleading with the men who were left there to guard me. None of the remaining men acted like they could hear me. In my assessment, this was it. I was staring down a true death sentence. I immediately began praying. If my mother, a devout Catholic, had taught me nothing else, she had definitely taught me how to pray.

"Hail Mary full of Grace . . ." I mumbled, closing my eyes and preparing for my impending death. As soon as I closed my eyes, I was thrust backward in my mind, reviewing how I'd ever let the gorgeous, smooth-talking Eduardo Santos get my gullible ass into this mess.